"My ██████████████████ **nily is**
getting ████████████████ **aid**

Rachel stood two steps above him on the porch, wearing a nightgown of some thin, summer material. "I'm going to forget you said that," she retorted.

"We're consenting adults."

"I'd never risk my reputation for some fast-talking, Yankee con artist."

"If you're not interested in anything I have to say, maybe you'll be interested in what I plan to do." Trey reached beneath her nightgown with both hands, stroking up the fullness of her bare calves.

Rachel gasped. This couldn't be happening. He was touching her exactly the way she longed to be touched. He pulled her down a step until she was straddling his thigh, his mouth on her breast.

Mindless with wanting, she felt the shattering of her vaunted self-control and the blossoming of passion she'd ruthlessly suppressed for so long.

"Let's go back to my place," Trey said in a strangled voice. "What I want from you—what I want to give you is going to take a long…slow…time…."

Dear Reader,

Temptation is Mills & Boon's sensuous romance series...a series for the 1990s! Fast-paced, humorous, adventurous, these stories are about men and women falling in love—and making the ultimate commitment.

Rebels & Rogues, our year-long salute to the Temptation hero, ends this month with THE RED-BLOODED YANKEE! Ruth Jean Dale has written about a footloose rogue who shies clear of family and commitment.

I hope you have enjoyed all twelve Rebels & Rogues books— stories of men who are rough around the edges, but incredibly sexy. Men full of charm, yet ready to fight for the love of a very special woman...

Look out for more terrific Temptation novels in 1994! If you would like to share your views on any of the Temptation stories then, please, take the time to write to me.

The Editor
Mills & Boon Temptation
Eton House
18-24 Paradise Road
Richmond
Surrey
TW9 1SR

The Red-Blooded Yankee!

MILLS & BOON LIMITED
ETON HOUSE, 18-24 PARADISE ROAD
RICHMOND, SURREY TW9 1SR

First published in Great Britain in 1993
by Mills & Boon Limited, Eton House, 18-24 Paradise Road,
Richmond, Surrey TW9 1SR

© Betty Duran 1992

ISBN 0 263 78529 7

21 - 9312

Made and printed in Great Britain

Prologue

ONLY A MANIAC with a death wish would try it.

Riding a horse at breakneck speed down a nearly sheer canyon wall in the middle of San Diego's Balboa Park was dumb enough; doing it in the middle of the night—blinded by beams of light flashed from a hovering helicopter while heading hell-bent into headlights and spotlights from a gaggle of police cars waiting below on the freeway—made it suicide.

That was what they all said, and Trey Smith supposed they might be right. But what the hell? He gave the buckskin a friendly slap on the neck. If it was easy, they wouldn't pay him to do it.

Automatically checking the saddle's double cinches, Trey eavesdropped on two nearby gofers. "Man, Trey Smith's really gone around the bend this time. Why didn't he let that new hotshot have the honor of breaking his neck on this stunt?"

Came the response in a deeper voice, "Who knows why Trey Smith does anything?"

Trey Smith himself didn't consider his motivation to be anybody's business but his own. No point advertising the fact that the kid had suffered an acute attack of good sense and sent his pregnant girlfriend to plead for him. She'd claimed the little jerk was laid up with the flu. Trey hadn't called her on it.

"Trey's an all right guy," the deeper of the two voices went on, "but he's as nuts as the rest of 'em. You can't be sane and make your living falling off buildings and crashing cars."

"Yeah. You'd think he'd learn after he tore hell out of his knee on that shoot in Arizona."

That was what you'd think, all right, even without knowing Trey was being considered for the stunt coordinator's job on that big picture coming up in Russia. A shame to risk it all for a smart-assed kid, but Trey found it hard to say no to a woman, even when she wasn't pregnant and begging.

"What the hell," the disembodied voice behind Trey announced. "If anybody can pull this off, he can. C'mon—I don't wanna miss anything. Let's get over there by the edge of the canyon where we can get a good view."

Trey shifted slightly to watch the two men walk away, heads together, gossiping like old ladies. Grinning as he turned back to the horse, his glance locked with that of an old man standing no more than six feet away. A shock something like recognition jolted Trey and he felt the smile disappear.

At first he thought the old guy must be a movie extra because he looked like the stereotypical cattle baron— well-cut Western suit, expensive black boots that could only be hand-tooled, wide white Stetson and a lined, sun-darkened face. The Marlboro man grown old, Trey thought, judging the man to be a hale and hearty octogenarian.

But if he was an extra, he'd wandered over here from the wrong set. This picture was a slam-bang action-adventure flick; the horse was incidental, added to make the hero look macho. The man was probably somebody's friend, Trey decided, curious to see how a make-believe cowboy compared with the real thing.

The old cowman removed his Stetson and shoved a hand through his wild white hair. He turned to the tall, hard-eyed young man beside him. "We found him, Jesse," he said, his accent all Texas twang, looking straight at Trey. "We by damn have finally found him."

What the hell was that supposed to mean? Trey's instinct said *find out*, but at the moment a helicopter swooped out of the night, its drone overpowering everything else. The buckskin flinched, then stood trembling beneath Trey's soothing hands.

Brilliant beams of light swept over the steep side of the canyon, revealing the brushy inclines in all their treachery. Excitement hummed through the crowd of onlookers and workers alike. An assistant director shouted orders; a flunky nodded and trotted over to Trey.

Trey shook him off, his attention on the jittery animal. The people, the lights, the confusion were nothing more than a minor and familiar irritation as he concentrated on the job. Holding the bridle with one hand, he stroked the horse's nose, leaning close to speak in a soothing voice.

Still, he heard the words drawled behind him: "So what you waitin' for? Let's get this over with." And the old man's response: "You loco? Last thing I want to do is disturb the boy's concentration just before he rides off a cliff." A pause, and then? "I can wait."

Trey spun around but the two men were walking away, slipping into the crowd and out of sight.

"You ready?" It was the stunt coordinator, wearing headphones and carrying a clipboard. He also wore an earring and dark glasses, but hey—this was California.

Trey raised one eyebrow and grimaced. "I was born ready." He thrust his left foot into the stirrup, then swung himself up and onto the buckskin. He wore athletic shoes instead of boots, matching the costume of the actor he was doubling. Too bad; if he lost a stirrup on the descent he'd play hell finding it again without the advantage of the proper footwear.

Easily controlling his excited horse, Trey grinned at the stunt coordinator. "Roll 'em," he advised, "'cause old Buck and I are only gonna do this once."

TREY SMITH slowly battled back to consciousness. Groggy, hurting, he struggled to open his eyes.

What the hell had happened?

The gag—he'd headed the buckskin over the lip of the cliff into the void, said a silent prayer and hung on. Trey had used the horse in other pictures and the animal had never let him down. Usually surefooted, the horse had strained for balance, fought to stay upright—then lights had hit both horse and rider square between the eyes.

What had happened next? He remembered underbrush snagging a stirrup, the horse's momentum nearly tearing his foot off . . . He groaned. Trying to remember took an enormous amount of effort.

Speaking took even more. "Where in the hell am . . . ?" He finally got his eyes open and his blurry gaze focused on a syringe big enough to stun an elephant. It was heading straight for him.

"Son of a bitch!" Trey threw himself out of the way, landing on hands and knees on a hard tile floor. Agony shot through him, so intense he nearly blacked out. His knee—he'd injured his goddamn knee again when the buckskin rolled over his leg. The brace hadn't been able to protect him, not from the effects of a twenty-foot tumble ending on highway asphalt.

Before he could catch his breath, hands grabbed him, lifted him, held him down. Was he having the nightmare again? "Dammit, no needles!" he roared, flailing at his attackers. "No drugs!"

The forward advance of the needle halted and Trey finally saw the threat—a young doctor, not the street punk he'd expected. Redheaded and freckled, the medic was also red-faced and angry.

"I've got to sew you together, blockhead!" he shouted.

"Then do it!" Light-headed with relief, Trey became aware of the slow ooze of something down the side of his head, something that could only be blood. "Do what you have to do, but you're not doping me up with your damned needles!"

So that was what the doctor did. Trey lay there, accepting the needle punching its way through his skin, the drag of sutures as the doctor made repairs—better pain than drug-induced oblivion. Stitches through his right eyebrow, more in his right shoulder and the right side of his neck....

The doctor knotted the last suture and Trey let out the breath he'd been holding. So did the doctor; he gave his patient a curiously respectful glance and dropped his equipment onto a tray. A nurse promptly picked it up and hurried out.

"Wait here while I find out what's keeping those X-rays," he ordered. "I don't think the original fall hurt that knee as much as your swan dive off the table. I may need more pictures."

"Whatever you say, Doc." Feeling fractionally better, Trey waited until the doctor had left, then pushed himself up and onto his elbows to look around the cubicle of the hospital emergency room. He saw a figure seated on a chair against the wall, the same handsome old man he'd noticed on the movie set just before everything went to hell.

Trey frowned. He didn't know this old guy from Adam. "Who in the hell," Trey croaked as politely as his dry throat would allow, "are you?"

A half grin touched the leathery old face. "Why, boy," the old man drawled, rising to his feet, "I'm your several times removed great-uncle Thom T. Taggart. You can call me Thom T."

"The hell you say." Trey swayed back on his bent arm, groggy and a little sick to his stomach. "You got the wrong man, cowboy. I don't have a relative in the world."

"Wrong. You're a Taggart."

Adrift in some surreal fog, Trey licked his lips. "I'm not a Taggart, I don't know any Taggarts, and I don't *want* to know any Taggarts. This is . . . clearly a case of mistaken identity."

"No, it ain't," the old man disagreed patiently. "I reckon this is quite a shock to you, but . . ."

Clearly the understatement of the year.

". . . it ain't no mistake. Ya see, about a year ago, I hired me a private detective in Dallas to find out what happened to the lost branch of the Taggart family tree. The trail started in 1876, and it's been like trackin' bees through a blizzard, but—"

"I'm not your man. I'm an orphan. From New York City."

"Yep. I know that and a helluva lot more. Like, before you got into the movies you was a United States Marine . . . a detective in Miami . . . punched cows in Wyoming a couple years till the winters got to you . . ." Thom T. ticked off the events of Trey's life on the fingers of one hand. "Bounced drunks in a nightclub in L.A. You've never been married but you do like the ladies." He winked.

Trey figured he must still be woozy with pain because the old guy was starting to scare him. "So what's your point?"

Thom T. leaned closer. "Just this. I ain't as young as I used to be. Before I meet my maker, I figure it's my duty to reunite the two branches of the Taggart family."

Exhausted and confused, Trey struggled to understand, and failed. In his present state, this was simply too much to take in. "So what are you doing *here?*" he finally managed.

"Ain't it obvious?" Thom T. Taggart looked nonplussed, as if he'd spelled it all out. "I've come to take you home to Texas."

1

TREY SMITH sat in the Alamo Cantina outside Showdown, Texas, nursing a nonalcoholic beer and wishing he were somewhere a little more friendly; dangling by a thread over a pit of vipers, for instance.

He'd been in the state of Texas for two days now and had met a solid wall of hostility. This had puzzled him until he realized everybody thought he was either some kind of con artist out to fleece a rich old man or just another crazy Californian.

"Damn Yankee" was the nicest thing he'd been called thus far, and he wasn't real sure how many times he'd be willing to hear it before taking appropriate action. He smiled darkly into his beer; who needed this grief? He was only here because he liked the old man and wanted to let him down easy, that and the fact he needed a place to recuperate from his latest injuries.

The stitches were healing nicely, but the knee was a bitch. Doctors had warned him months ago that it needed surgery but he'd put them off. If he didn't follow orders this time and give it a chance to mend completely, there was no telling what kind of trouble he'd be in.

Thom T. Taggart had played shamelessly on Trey's apprehensions on that score to get him to agree to convalesce in Texas. "You don't wanna end up a cripple, do you?" the old man had demanded. "It'll be that or surgery if you ain't careful. The way you bucked when that doc come at you, I reckon it's safe to assume you don't want to go under the knife."

It wasn't the knife Trey feared, but he didn't say so.

Thom T. looked pleased. "That's what I thought," he said smugly. "C'mon back to Texas for a good, long rest. Whatta you got to lose? Besides, I ain't gonna take no for an answer, now that we found you."

"We, hell." Jesse Taggart, the tall man who'd been with Thom T. on the movie set, had interrupted. "*You* found him, Grandpa, you and your expensive snoop, and I'm not convinced this is really him. Why the hell you'd go through so much trouble to dig up some Yankee shirttail relation . . ."

"Simmer down, boy." Thom T. waved off his grandson's reservations. He fixed Trey with a narrow-eyed gaze. "You're Taggart blood and I don't give a hoot in hell who thinks otherwise."

Trey thought otherwise and said so. The evidence linking him to the Taggarts was more circumstantial than conclusive but Thom T. didn't see it that way, relying instead on the detective's last words: "My gut instinct tells me Trey Smith is your man, and I think the facts will support me once I finish processing all the data I've collected."

Unfortunately, the detective had hung up the telephone, walked out the door and collapsed with a heart attack. The man's widow was forwarding material to Thom T. piecemeal as she found it, but the old man had been too impatient to wait. So here Trey was in Texas, a fish out of water in more ways than one.

Restlessness had brought him to the Alamo Cantina this Friday night in August. He'd borrowed Thom T.'s

Ford pickup. To be accurate, he'd *taken* Thom T.'s pickup and left a note, since the old man had gone out to dinner with his grandson Jesse, Jesse's good-looking wife Meg and their kid, whatever his name was. They'd invited Trey to join them, but he'd declined, so they'd have a chance to talk about him.

Check that. He'd declined to give Jesse another shot at persuading the old man that Trey might be a lot of things, but a Taggart he wasn't.

Trey didn't see what was so hot about being a Taggart. He'd grown up a loner. His only experience in "belonging" had been a stint in the Marine Corps, where loners and outsiders could prosper if they were tough enough . . . and Trey was.

After the Taggarts drove away in Thom T.'s Cadillac, Trey had hot-wired the pickup on an impulse and taken off to scout the area. Eventually he'd stopped here, for a drink he didn't particularly want with people who clearly didn't like him. Maybe he'd had visions of a rowdy honky-tonk with a lot of friendly hicks a-drinkin', a-dancin' and just a-waitin' to make a stranger feel welcome.

They were a-drinkin' and a-dancin', all right, but nobody was a-waitin' to do anything for a stranger—maybe *to* him but not *for* him. Could it have anything to do with Trey's khaki shorts, UC Berkeley T-shirt and goofy California sandals in an establishment chock-full of denim and pointy-toed boots?

Nah, he assured himself, tongue firmly in cheek. So he'd grabbed a phony brew at the bar—only after the waitress in a short cowgirl suit had made it abundantly clear that she never intended to glance his way even if he sat there patiently for thirty years—and carried it to a table.

It was a hell of a scene for a city boy. On a sawdust-covered dance floor, sweaty no-neck cowboys and no-collar workers with sleeves rolled up to reveal hairy arms tripped the light fantastic with high-haired cowgirls wearing enough makeup to stun a Hollywood director.

The opening of the outside door disturbed Trey's concentration and he glanced around, did a double take and sat up straight. There stood a sight worth seeing in a murky Texas bar at nine o'clock at night; a beautiful woman wearing oversize dark glasses. In California he'd chalk it up to drugs or terminal cool without a second thought. But here in the Alamo Cantina, with a portrait of John Wayne as Davy Crockett glaring down?

She hesitated just inside the door and he found himself watching with growing interest, which, he supposed, said something about Texas women. So far it seemed they all had high hair, funny accents and boyfriends called Bubba.

Holding his glass in the curve of one hand, he looked the newcomer over with a connoisseur's eye. Her hair fascinated him. That was a surprise, since hair didn't figure prominently on his list of female attributes. But hers was really something, dark and thick, curling wildly around an oval face before it tumbled over her shoulders. There was something elemental about that hair, and Trey found himself contemplating how it would look spread out over a pillow.

His pillow.

He grinned, feeling more like himself than he had since he'd entered this accursed state. The only thing he liked better than fighting was loving, and the Alamo Cantina now held the potential for both.

His leisurely perusal continued. Mid-twenties, he decided, maybe younger. Tight jeans caressed rounded hips and long, sexy legs; a snug-fitting cowboy shirt didn't leave a hell of a lot to the imagination.

Especially when she drew a quick breath and glanced around. Her gaze locked with his frankly appraising one—or would have, had her eyes not been concealed behind the glasses. Even so, he knew she was looking at him. She held the contact for a few seconds, then pulled away with a toss of her head and a curl of her lush, red lips.

Trey settled back in his chair and watched her walk toward the bar. She glanced around as she moved between the tables, obviously looking for someone. While Trey stared, she pushed one finger awkwardly against the nosepiece of her glasses to reposition them.

That told him the glasses were worn either as part of a disguise or to conceal something. A black eye? Was she involved in an abusive relationship? He hoped not. Any man who would lift his hand against a woman didn't deserve to live.

The waitress, leaning over a table to deliver drinks, straightened and in so doing, managed to bump into the newcomer. The woman jerked back and her glasses tumbled to the floor. Trey had just a quick look at her face before she snatched up the glasses and clapped them back into place, but it was long enough to eliminate abuse as a motivation.

"Sorry, honey." The waitress offered a helping hand. "Yawl okay?"

"I'm fine."

A low, slightly breathless voice. Sexy.

The waitress grinned and moved on without any sign of recognition. So the woman with the curly hair and great bod was a mystery woman, indeed. Well, well, well . . . things were looking up.

The woman reached the bar. Leaning across an empty stool, she said something to the bartender. He gave her a quick once-over, grinned, shook his head and proceeded to draw a draft.

She was one damned sexy female all right, Trey thought, admiring the curve of her backside. He was definitely in the market for a woman like that.

The way he looked at it, there were two kinds of women: the good-time girls—his personal favorites— and the martyrs, the "good" ones who sucked all the joy out of life, loaded down a man with guilt and then whined because he was never at home. The fact that this woman, provocatively dressed as she was, would walk into a bar alone, order a beer and check out the clientele, told Trey all he needed to know.

There was one slight problem, however. Where the hell would he take her once he picked her up? Not back to that damned ranch—Falling-Over-T's or whatever they called it. Although Thom T. did seem like a savvy old gent. Maybe . . .

Nah, he was too old-fashioned. If she didn't invite Trey to her place, maybe he could sneak her into one of the ranch's empty outbuildings. . . . He laughed out loud at the thought.

She glanced at him for the second time, and he felt her disapproval almost as if she were privy to his thoughts. He gave her his most charming *we're-both-interested-why-don't-you-admit-it?* smile, but all he got for his trouble was another arrogant toss of her dark, luxurious mane before she turned to accept her beer.

Playing hard to get huh? Trey felt the competitive juices begin to flow.

The beefy man on the bar stool nearest her set down his long-neck beer and leaned close. "Howdy, honey," he drawled, looking her over with explicit approval. "Lookin' for someone? Have a little set-down and tell me all about it. Helpin' little gals is my speci-ality." He patted the empty stool in front of her.

"I'll just bet it is," she said skeptically. "On second thought, maybe you can help. I'm lookin' for Laddy Cox. Yawl know him?"

Shit. She was taken. Trey frowned into his beer. But how taken? He brightened; anything short of marriage was all right with him. Maybe this Laddy wouldn't even show up.

The clown at the bar wrinkled his forehead in a parody of thought. "I know him, but he ain't been here tonight. How 'bout ol' Jimbo keeps you company while you wait?"

"Thanks, but no thank—"

He made a grab for her and she stepped away, a little clumsily. Despite her come-hither looks, she didn't appear adept at playing bar games. She looked around uncertainly, which was clearly the opening Jimbo needed; he slipped an arm around her waist and dragged her onto the bar stool.

The bartender gave the man and woman a bored glance, dropped his towel and walked through a door behind the bar. If there was trouble, he apparently wanted no part of it. The woman could expect no help from that quarter, and no one else in the room even seemed to notice.

Except Trey. He set his beer aside. *Come on, Jimbo. Make a pest of yourself!*

The woman tried to push Jimbo away without declaring all-out war. She obviously didn't want to draw attention to herself; she kept glancing around as if to make sure no one was watching while at the same time slapping at the man's hands. Maybe she still thought there was a chance of getting out of this without making a total spectacle of herself.

There wasn't. Jimbo leaned close, his grin lusty. "So what's yore name, good-lookin'? Don't believe I've ever seen you around these here parts."

"You *haven't*, you gargantuan buffoon!" Her accent magically disappeared and she gave him another ineffectual shove. "Will you *please* take your hands off me before . . . before . . ." She was panting, apparently unable to think of a threat he might believe or that she could enforce.

"Before what, pretty baby?" Jimbo hugged her tighter, gloating at her inability to dislodge him. "How about you 'n' me gettin' a little better acquainted?"

That's my cue, Trey thought, standing up. He stepped forward, putting one hand on the woman's shoulder and the other hand on Jimbo's—not so lightly. "Listen to what the lady says, big guy. Otherwise you'll be putting yourself in a potentially dangerous situation." He said it pleasantly, hopefully.

Jimbo glared into the eyes of this interloper. "Butt out, sissy-dresser." He looked Trey over, taking in the California chic with undisguised scorn. In all likelihood Trey's stubbly, unshaven jaw was of no interest, but the stitches poking through the partly healed gash above his right eyebrow must have been. Jimbo's eyes widened, then narrowed.

But he didn't seem prepared to back off, not quite yet, adding in a blustery aside to the woman; "Damn Yankee's gonna get hisself in a peck'a trouble if he don't learn to mind his man—"

Jimbo's words ended in a squawk of surprise; he grabbed at the hand suddenly clamped around his throat. Trey ignored the man's struggles and smiled gently at the woman. "I think he's sorry. In case he's not, or in the unlikely event that he has friends, would you care to join me at my table to wait for your . . . ah . . . whatever?"

She looked to be on the verge of refusing, then glanced Jimbo's way and gasped. "Yes! Just let him go!"

"Sure. Sorry about that." Trey unwrapped his fingers, for all the world as if he'd forgotten ever putting them around the brawny throat. Flexing his hands, he gave her an innocent smile, the one he knew always served him well.

She slid off the bar stool, in her haste apparently misjudging his nearness. The breasts beneath the Western-cut shirt brushed against the inner surface of his bare forearm.

Damn! Excitement clenched Trey's gut and wiped the calculated smile off his face. This woman was dynamite! Sex with her might even restore the tarnished glory of Texas womanhood.

Jimbo, gasping and choking, sat on his bar stool rubbing his throat. The whole thing had gone down so quickly that no one else in the bar seemed aware that anything had happened.

"You son of a—you—you damn . . ."

Trey patted Jimbo's shoulder reassuringly. "Yeah, I know—damn Yankee," he supplied, and turned to follow the trim little backside to his table.

The woman sat down facing the door and placed her untouched beer upon the table. She did not smile. "Thank you," she said without looking at him.

Trey frowned, wishing they were past all this bullshit so they could get on to the real stuff. He was getting too excited too fast. He wondered how it was going to feel to thrust his hands through that wild tangle of curls. Would her nipples be large or small, dusky rose or ruby red?

He swallowed with difficulty and tried to ignore the clamoring of his body. It had been too long between women, that was all. Since he'd chosen to ignore Deb's ultimatum last spring, he'd been without a reliable source of sex.

Hell of a way to live.

The woman was frowning at him. He had to say something, so he said, "What did you say?"

She smiled and it was the first sincere expression of amusement he'd seen from her. There was something both shy and inviting in that smile and the effect dazzled him. Damn those glasses, he wanted to see her eyes!

"I was thankin' you, that's all."

"It was nothing." He brushed it aside with a modesty he knew was becoming. "I was kind of hoping he'd insist. But never mind that. What's your name?"

She looked taken aback. "Wh-why, it's..." She licked her lips and looked away, which was just as well, because he couldn't stop himself staring at the gleam of moisture left behind by that flick of her tongue. "You can call me Liz," she said finally in that slightly breathless little voice.

He pulled his gaze from her mouth, waiting for her to ask his name in return. She didn't, just kept looking around the room as if she thought the Laddy guy was hiding behind a chair or somewhere.

Trey was growing irritated by her refusal to acknowledge the connection that hummed so clearly between them. Ignoring it wasn't going to make it go away. Maybe if he could get her talking... "So do you live around here?" he asked.

"No." She didn't offer to tell him where she *did* live. After a moment she added, "You?" without real interest.

"I'm a native," he said. "Can't you tell?"

She gave him a startled glance, then seemed to recognize the sarcasm. She looked down at her hands in her lap. "Oh," she said helplessly. "You're kiddin', right?"

There was something so defenseless and appealing in the way she spoke that Trey's curiosity doubled. Her manner was completely at odds with the big black glasses, the lavishly applied makeup and provocative clothing, but the body he glimpsed beneath all that was the real thing. She was both a mystery and a challenge, two things he dearly loved.

He tried again. "Yeah, I'm kidding." Now what? He glanced around at the room. "I'd ask you to dance but I've got a bum knee," he offered.

"I noticed the stitches above your eye." She nodded toward them. "Were you in an accident?"

"You could say that." He dredged up a suffering-but-brave expression.

"What happened?"

He thought he heard the faintest note of interest. "Horse threw me," he said, sure she'd recognize stoic understatement.

She laughed. "Really? I didn't take you for a cow-boy."

He liked the way she looked him over when she said it. *Now we're getting somewhere,* he thought. Time to hit her with the magic word: Hollywood. "I'm not," he said modestly. "I'm actually a—"

One minute she was listening with interest, the next he might as well have been speaking a foreign language. Turning in his chair, he saw the much-anticipated Laddy Cox.

Hell, he couldn't be a day over twenty-one, way too young for the hot little number rising to go to him. And drunk, to boot. The kid wavered in the open doorway, a foolish grin on his face, letting out all the air-conditioning.

"Close the damned door!" at least a dozen voices chorused.

"Don't get your bowels in a' uproar." The boy took a staggering step and violently banged the door shut with one booted foot.

"Laddy!"

Liz started forward but Trey caught her arm in warning. Beating up doors was one thing, beating up women quite another. Best to see which way young Master Cox would fall.

Laddy saw Liz and a flush darkened his already florid cheeks. "Ah, go home, Lizzie!" he yelled. "Lemme alone for once, why don'cha?"

Stumbling to the bar, the boy leaned over the same empty stool where Liz had stood. "Beertender, gimme a bar!" he yelled, then burst into laughter at his own wit.

The bartender, the same one who'd looked the other way earlier, continued polishing a beer stein with a towel. "Shove off, kid," he said finally. "You're drunk."

"So?" The kid thrust out his jaw at a pugnacious angle.

"So I'll tell you the same thing I useta tell your old man—I don't serve drunks, especially them that comes in lookin' for trouble."

"I wanna beer!" Laddy banged his fist against the bar; people were beginning to give him disapproving glances.

Liz shook off Trey's hand and hurried to the boy's side. She caught his elbow. "Laddy, you've got to come home."

Shit, she lives with this little turd?

"Get away from me, Lizzie." Laddy tried to shake her off but she hung on. "Can't a man have a beer without everybody ganging up on him?"

"A *man* can, sonny."

Jimbo heaved himself around on his bar stool. His narrow eyes looked mean and unhappy. Trey wondered if the big clown had been drinking and thinking about what a weenie he was. Maybe he thought he'd just found somebody he could cut down to size.

As far as Trey was concerned, that was fine. He didn't owe a dumb, drunk kid any consideration, especially when said kid had a lock on the woman Trey had set his own sights on. As a matter of fact, he half hoped Jimbo would beat the hell out of the little twerp.

Seeing the handwriting on the wall, Trey settled back in his chair and prepared to enjoy what was coming.

Laddy stuck that square jaw into Jimbo's face. "You sayin' I ain't a man?"

Jimbo stood up; he was at least eight inches taller than Laddy. "I'm sayin' you're a dumb, drunk kid. . . ."

My thoughts exactly.

"And you oughta appreciate this little gal's concern."

Yeah, you ungrateful little prick.

"And run along home with her like a good little boy."

Hey, wait a minute—don't go too far! I got plans for her myself.

"That's what I thought you meant."

The kid flung up his right arm and banged into Liz. She uttered a little cry and stumbled back on the excessively high heels of her boots, bumping into a man who'd come up behind her to see what was going on.

In fact, the disagreement was drawing a lot of attention. Drinkers, even dancers were drifting over.

The cocktail waitress in the Dale Evans suit, passing by with a tray full of drinks, stopped short. "Hey!" she cried. "Whatta you think you're doin', Laddy Cox? Nobody hits a woman in the Alamo!"

With that she hauled back her tray, letting the drinks fly where they would, and smacked him in the shoulder with it.

Her blow knocked the boy aside just in time. Jimbo let loose with a roundhouse right. The blow whistled over the kid's shoulder and connected with the chin of the man who'd helped Liz regain her balance.

The newcomer, a construction worker, from the rough-edged look of him, howled. "Who the hell you think you're beatin' on, Jimbo, you jackass? I'll teach you to—" He punctuated his words with a blow to Jimbo's solar plexus.

The brawl was on.

Trey's hands itched to curl into fists and get in a few licks but he held back. He was a sick man, he reminded himself piously. He was in Texas to recuperate. He couldn't afford to delay his recovery, not if he still intended to be physically fit to work on that picture in Russia in January—and he damned sure did.

But Liz was still hanging on Laddy's arm, trying to drag him toward the back door. Trey shifted unhappily in his chair; she was going to get hurt if she didn't get out of the way. Look at the waitress; after she'd lambasted the kid she'd had the good sense to take her tray and climb to safety on top of the bar. Once there, she could lean over in comparative safety to bop unwary heads.

Other women squealed and pranced around the fringes of the uproar, but not Liz. She had to get right in the middle of the fray. Damn that kid! Didn't he know a good thing when he had one?

Trey jumped to his feet and started forward; his leg buckled and he stopped. *Don't do it—it's not worth it.*

He sat down on the nearest chair and rubbed his throbbing knee.

The boy went down and took Liz with him. Through the constantly moving forest of denim-blue legs, Trey saw her grab the kid's lapels and lean over, giving him hell, no doubt. He deserved it.

Jimbo stumbled within reach of the waitress; she brought her tray crashing down on his head. His eyes opened wide and he toppled like giant oak, his falling body missing Liz by a whisker.

Dammit, this had gone too far! Trey jumped to his feet and felt himself sway. He didn't give a damn what happened to the boy, but he was dragging Liz out of harm's way before she got herself killed.

Ducking a flying fist, he leaned forward, caught her beneath the arms and lifted her. Neither her shrieks nor her struggles deterred him. He hauled her up, wrestling her away from the fallen boy.

Turning her to face him, he leaned close to be heard. "Liz, stop it! I'm getting you out of here before you get your pretty little—"

He stopped short, realizing with a sense of shock that her glasses had been lost somewhere in the melee. He saw a furious flash of hazel eyes in a face alive with passion—just before a hand grabbed the ribbing of his T-shirt and hauled him around to meet its mate.

Fierce joy surged through Trey. He'd tried, he'd really tried, but the decision had been taken out of his hands. He blocked the next punch and threw one of his own. His attacker doubled up with a grunt and slid to the floor, immediately lost in the sea of boots.

Where was she? A broad back in a cowboy shirt blocked his view, so Trey reached out to give it a delicate tap. The man turned just in time to get acquainted with Trey's fist.

But where was Liz? For that matter, where the hell was Laddy? Wading through the opposition, it took Trey a long time to realize they were both gone.

2

"HEY, LIGHTEN UP, will you?" Trey ducked away from Meg Taggart. He didn't need first aid for a couple of scrapes and a little bleeding, even from a woman as good-looking as Jesse Taggart's wife. He saw he'd offended her and added defensively, "It's not life threatening."

"Yeah, Meggie," Thom T. chimed in, indicating Trey's battered face. "It's a long way from his heart." The old guy chuckled; he seemed gratified rather than angered by Trey's misadventure earlier in the evening.

Meg's small hands felt gentle on Trey's cheeks. "But some of the stitches have come loose," she objected in her cultured Bostonian accent. "You really should see a doctor. Your scar may be worse if you don't."

Trey kept his gaze level. "So?"

Her soft mouth pursed; then she let out her breath in a disgusted whoosh. "Men! You're all alike!" She threw the dripping cloth back into the pan of water and glared at her husband, who hadn't said a word. "Go ahead, take his side!"

Jesse shrugged. "What can I say? He's a grown man, Meggy. He can take his own lumps."

"Fine. In that case, I wash my hands of the lot of you!"

Meg marched out of the room, back straight and head held high. The three men said nothing for a count of ten, then Jesse burst out laughing while Thom T. chortled and pounded on Trey's shoulder—the one with all the stitches beneath the ripped and bloody T-shirt.

Trey laughed with them. When they'd settled down, he asked in a voice he knew wasn't as casual as he'd have liked, "Either of you know a woman called Liz or maybe Lizzie?"

"Woman, huh?" Thom T. grinned.

"Lizzie." Jesse considered. "There's Lizzie Goodfellow."

Trey picked up the cloth Meg had left behind and squeezed it out over the pan. "Real looker. Mid-twenties, tall, lots of dark curly hair, great bod. Runs with a kid named Laddy Cox."

Thom T. grunted. "Laddy, huh! He's a wild 'un. No tellin' who he's took up with. Last I heard it was a little gal from over ta Crystal Springs." His glance grew shrewd. "How strong's your interest in this Lizzie?"

"Not very," Trey lied. In fact, his interest was stronger than ever. On top of everything else, he owed her for that clip on the jaw.

"Good," Jesse interjected, "because I got something more important we all need to talk about before I take Meg and the boy to Boston tomorrow." He walked to a well-stocked bar cart. "Drink? How about you, Thom T.?"

"Don't believe I will, son," the old rancher declined.

Trey shook his head and pressed the cloth to the throbbing area above his eye.

Jesse poured for himself, watching Trey. "Not much of a drinker, are you."

Trey shrugged. "Alcohol's just another drug. I don't like to put junk in my body." Uncomfortable with this turn in the conversation, he threw the cloth back into the pan. It hit with a splash that dampened the antique table. "You want to talk about the truck? I left a note."

Thom T.'s bushy white eyebrows soared. "The truck?"

"I did hot-wire it," Trey persisted.

"What for?"

"To start it." Trey struggled for patience.

"You coulda just used the key. When it's not in the ignition, we leave it hangin' on a nail on the back porch. Ever'body in the country knows they's welcome to drive anything I got."

Incredulous, Trey started to laugh, then saw the old man was serious and stopped.

"It's not about the truck," Jesse resumed. "It's about what happens after I leave for Boston tomorrow."

"What? Ahh, I get it. You don't want to leave your grandfather alone with someone who may be an impostor or a con artist."

Jesse raised his brows and dipped his chin in acquiescence. "Something like that," he agreed calmly.

"Hell, I *am* an impostor, only it was his idea, not mine." *How many times was he going to have to go through this?* He'd told them before they ever left California, told them forty times he wasn't the person they were looking for.

"I only came along for the ride and you damned well know it," he reminded Jesse. "I was hurting and the old guy took advantage of me." Trey darted Thom T. an accusing glance.

"Yeah, I know," Jesse conceded. "But since I don't know how well you're gonna handle temptation, I've

decided to bring someone else in here to stay a while just
to see how things go."

"No dice." Trey eyed Jesse coldly. Many men flinched
from such a challenge; Jesse didn't. "I told you I don't
like the whole damned world knowing my business,
especially when my business makes me look like some
kind of damned opportunist."

"Now, boy, nobody said—"

"Forget it, Thom T. You know I'm right. Hell, *I*
wouldn't trust me if I was you."

The old man looked crestfallen, which made Trey feel
like a jerk, but he couldn't relent.

"I trust you," Thom T. said. "You're family."

"No, I'm not."

"Don't you *want* a family?" the old man asked
plaintively.

"How the hell would I know? I never had one." Once
Trey had wanted a family more than anything in the
world, but he'd long since given up that dream. He'd
been a loner for a long time now, and he liked it that
way. At least, he'd thought so until the Taggarts came
roaring into his life, turning everything upside down.

Hell, he didn't know how he felt about anything
anymore. Turning back to Jesse he added, "About
moving someone else into the house—wouldn't it be
easier for me just to move out?"

"No!" Thom T. stomped a booted foot for emphasis.

"You sayin' you want to leave?" Jesse's brows rose.

Trey couldn't tell how Jesse felt about the matter from
his expression; not that it mattered. "That's right. Leave
the big house and move into the bunkhouse. How does
that strike you?"

The two men, so near in age and strength, so far apart in experience, stared at each other for a moment, and Trey felt a sort of silent understanding pass between them. Jesse began to smile, and Trey did likewise.

"You'll be more comfortable in the foreman's house," Jesse suggested softly. "It's just over that ridge to the west. Got its own road leadin' to the highway, nice and private . . . if that matters."

Trey grinned. "It matters. So you still want someone to move in here?"

Jesse glanced at his grandfather. "Yep. Friend of the family. She's the local librarian, and Thom T's going to ask her to sort everything out and draw a few conclusions. Not just about you, but the family legend as well. There's more at stake here than you know." He paused significantly, then added, "It'll be easier if she's right here, where she can get at everything."

Just what he needed, Trey thought; some old maid of a librarian hanging around, asking a lot of questions. At least he wouldn't be living under the same roof with her. *Watch out, Lizzie!* "And at the same time she can make sure I don't take off with the family silver."

Jesse shrugged. "You got that right."

"You'll like Rachel," Thom T. hurried to interject. "Her boy, too—nice kid, even if he is a little tame."

"Tame?" Trey raised his eyebrows.

"You know what they say—the wilder the colt, the better the horse."

Trey laughed. "No, don't think I ever heard anybody say that."

"Well it's true and you heard it now. Rachel's boy's twelve, thirteen, somethin' like that."

Rachel. Fuddy-duddy name. If she had a kid, she must be a widow. Librarians in dinky little Texas towns had to be too stodgy to get divorced.

"I don't care if he's a nice kid or not," Trey announced, "since I don't plan to adopt him."

Or the Taggarts, either.

RACHEL SAT at the kitchen table, ignoring the beginnings of a glorious, golden morning outside her window. All she could think about was the riot last night at the Alamo Cantina, and of the craven way she'd sneaked out the back door with her errant brother, leaving that tall, good-looking Yankee knee-deep in trouble.

She wondered if he'd got out of it all right. Probably; he'd struck her as a man who could take care of himself—and her, too, if she wasn't careful. Still, she couldn't seem to stop thinking about him; who he was . . . what he was . . . and why his sassy, sexy manner had disturbed her so.

Laddy stumbled into the kitchen and she watched him reach a shaking hand for the coffeepot.

"You broke your promise," she said tiredly.

Laddy poured, sloshing coffee onto the counter. He took a sip, burned his tongue and grimaced. He really did look like hell—in need of a shave, dark circles under his eyes, shirttail hanging outside his Levi's, bare feet.

"It wasn't exactly a promise," he hedged.

"It *was* a promise. You told me that if you started drinking you wouldn't drive—"

"I didn't drive!" Anger flashed in his hazel eyes. He walked to the table on wobbly legs and sank into the chair across from hers.

"Only because Virgil took your car keys away from you. He thought you'd bummed a ride to the Yellow Rose...."

"Yeah, well, I didn't." He refused to meet her glance, choosing to stare sullenly out the window. "Get off my back, will ya? I didn't drive. What's the big deal?"

Rachel wanted to put her head down upon her arms and bawl. She was tired of trying to reason with her brother about his drinking. Still, she never doubted she'd find a way to reach him. He *would not* end up like their father, the town drunk, head of his own clan of poor white trash.

Dammit, she'd worked too hard to overcome that stigma! With Thom T.'s help, she'd pulled herself up by the bootstraps. She would not let anyone drag her down again, nor her son or brother, either. No one in this town would ever find further fault with the morals of the Coxes, even if it meant strict adherence to an impossibly high standard.

Suddenly Laddy grinned. It did wonderful things to his face; he was an extremely handsome young man when he wasn't scowling or drinking. "Was I dreamin', or were you wearin' sunglasses in that dark honky-tonk in the middle of the night?"

"I didn't want anyone to recognize me," she said stiffly, feeling her cheeks flush with embarrassment.

"Why the hell not? This town knows by now what a Goody Two Shoes you are, Lizzie. It wouldn't ruin your reputation if you walked into a bar and ordered a beer. Normal people do it all the time."

"Shut up, Laddy. You don't know a thing about it. Everybody's just waiting for me to screw up. Hell will freeze over before I give them that satisfaction."

"Then at least admit you like puttin' one over on 'em. You like puttin' on your cowgirl suit and pullin' me out of bars. You've still got the family wild streak and every so often you've just gotta break out. Hell, it's the only fun you have anymore."

Cold dread filled her at the thought that there might be even a tiny grain of truth in what he said. The older she got, the more she worried about what her mother used to call "that wild Cox blood."

"I have plenty of fun," she lied, jumping up. "Want anything to eat? I'm about to start Jason's breakfast and I can—"

"God, no!" He looked horrified. "All I want is about a gallon of coffee before I head back to bed." He took another shaky gulp. "You workin' today?"

She nodded. "Library closes at two. Will you be here when I get home?"

"Sure." His head sagged; he looked as if he might fall asleep right there at the table.

Still, she wasn't satisfied; he'd broken the last promise he'd made to her, hadn't he? "It's important, Laddy. We've really got to talk about what happened last night."

"I said I would! Get off my back!"

She watched him stalk out of the kitchen, wondering what she could possibly say or do that would make a difference.

RACHEL POURED pancake batter onto the griddle, then glanced at Jesse. "Sure you won't have a short stack?" she invited.

He grinned over his coffee cup. "No, thanks, don't have time to talk and eat both. Give 'em to the champ."

He ruffled the hair of thirteen-year-old Jason, sitting at the breakfast table with his face in a book. The boy gave the man an absent smile and returned to his reading.

"Suit yourself." Rachel wielded the spatula expertly, flipping the golden-brown cakes without a bobble. "So what brings you out so early on a Saturday, J.J.?"

Jesse sighed and stared into his coffee cup. After a moment he said, "It's complicated." He looked meaningfully at Jason. "Think after you finish cooking the flapjacks we could maybe take a little walk?"

"Sure." Curious by now, she turned her attention back to the pancakes, quickly amassing a plateful for her son. She couldn't imagine what Jesse might want to talk about that Jason shouldn't hear, but she felt no sense of foreboding.

She plunked the plate loaded with pancakes in front of her son. "Think this'll do it, honey?"

"Fine, Mom, yeah, thanks." Without taking his eyes from the page, the boy reached out, rolled a pancake into a tube and stuck one end into his mouth.

Rachel looked at him for a moment, torn between pride in his intellectual abilities and despair over his lack of interest in anything else. She sighed and turned toward Jesse.

"Grab your coffee cup and let's go, cowboy," she said.

THEY SAT SIDE BY SIDE on swings tied in a big old oak tree in the backyard of Rachel's small house in Showdown. Her father had put up the swings many years ago, when Rachel was younger than Jason was now. He'd done it during one of his intermittent forays into sobriety, forays that had become less and less frequent as time went by.

She smoothed her navy-blue skirt over her knees; she'd be leaving for the library soon and was already dressed, her unruly hair slicked back in a dignified twist and light, conservative makeup applied. Laddy called her low-heeled dark pumps "Minnie Mouse shoes," but she didn't care; they were comfortable and unobtrusive. "So how's Thom T.?" she asked at last.

"Fine."

"He's been away."

"Yes." Jess drained his cup and held it between his knees. He started to speak, then stopped.

Rachel felt sudden alarm. She'd known Jessie all her life—she'd known all the Taggarts all her life—but she'd never seen him at a loss for words. If it wasn't Thom T.... "Jesse, is Boone all right?"

"Boone?" He looked up, surprise plain on his face. "He's fine, far as I know. Still in London."

"If it's not your brother and it's not your grandpa, and you already told me your wife and son are okay, what on earth is bothering you?" She gave a little push with her feet to start the swing moving.

"I might as well say it right out." He drew a deep breath. "He found him."

"Pronoun problems. Who found whom?"

"Thom T. found the man he believes is the last in Rose Taggart's line. He's out at the Rocking T right now."

"Good Lord!" Rachel slammed her feet into the ground to stop the swing.

"Rachel, looks like Showdown Days may be a lie. At least, the legend it's based on is in doubt. Rose Taggart didn't run away with the sheriff, she took off with that mangy gunfighter."

"You're kidding!" Rachel stared at him in astonishment. "If this is true . . . My gosh, the entire legend is false? I mean, you always know there's some license taken but if the whole thing is built on a lie... The town got its *name* from the showdown between Sheriff Jack and Boone the Mysterious Gunfighter! *Who's buried in the graveyard under that tombstone?*"

"God only knows, but apparently somebody other than the not-so-mysterious gunfighter," Jesse said mournfully. "His name was Boone Smith, by the way. Jeremy Edward Boone Smith, to be precise. Jeb Smith later on, when he and Rose got to California and married."

Shocked to the core, Rachel considered the ramifications of this news. "This has got to be a mistake," she decided. "If a rumor like this gets out it'll ruin the town. Do you have any idea how much money comes into our local economy each July during the Showdown Days shindig?"

"A lot." Jesse shifted uncomfortably on his wooden swing seat. "I'm pretty sure what I just told you is true, but not a hundred percent. That's where you come in."

"Me! What can *I* do?"

"Figure the whole thing out, Rachel. For the sake of the town, and for Thom T., too. He's bound and determined to welcome this stranger into the family, and

I'll tell you the truth, I don't know whether the guy's an impostor or not."

"An impostor is a person who pretends to be someone he's not for purposes of fraud," she said slowly. "Are you telling me you think the man Thom T.'s taken in is some kind of . . . crook? That he was somehow in cahoots with Thom T.'s private detective in perpetrating a fraud?"

Jesse's lean face wore a serious expression. "I'm tellin' you I don't know. I do know Thom T.'s already written that Yankee into his will, equal shares with me and Boone. I don't need Grandpa's money and I don't give a hoot who gets it, but I'd hate to see the old man hoodwinked."

"Then the Yankee could be a fortune hunter on top of everything else."

Jesse shrugged. "Who the hell knows? I'm askin' you to take a fair and impartial look at the whole situation...for Thom T's sake." He dumped the dregs in his cup onto the ground. "I'm takin' Meg and Randy to Boston today. Her grandpa was expectin' us a week ago and it'll be my hide if there's any more delay. I figured I had to go to California with Thom T. to see this Yankee, and she understood that, but her patience is at its limit."

Rachel nodded her understanding. "What do you think of him on a personal level?"

Jesse shrugged. "Hell, I like him—but I don't necessarily trust him. I should stay here and find out the truth for myself, but Meg and I . . ."

His voice trailed off and Rachel finished for him. "Just got back together and you don't want to mess things up again." Like everyone else in town, she knew about the long estrangement between Jesse and his Yankee wife. She also knew how miserable he'd been.

He looked relieved. "Yeah, that's about it. If I thought the old man was in any real trouble . . . I mean, Trey's not going to *hurt* him, physically, anyway."

Rachel nodded. "Okay then, let's get this straight. You want me to keep quiet about all this for the moment, I take it."

"Hell, yes!"

"And you want me to . . . what? Sift through all the materials Thom T.'s received from the detective, and the Taggart family papers, and see if a clear-cut answer emerges as to this guy's identity *and* to whether or not the entire legend is a crock? Have I got that right?"

Jesse nodded. "I always liked a bright woman," he teased.

"Yes, but not enough." She laughed; she'd had a crush on Jesse once, many long years ago. He'd never known, because she'd had Jason to worry about and because a Cox could hardly aspire to a Taggart. "Last, but not least, you want me to keep an eye on things at the Rocking T, just in case this guy is up to something funny. Have I got it all?"

"Just about." Jesse looked considerably more cheerful than when he'd arrived. "Mostly I want you to look out for Thom T. The only way you can do that properly is to move out to the ranch—with Jason, of course."

He jumped to his feet and beamed at her. "So when can you move in?"

TREY RUBBED the buckskin's velvety muzzle, murmuring sweet nothings into the horse's ear. He looked across the animal's back at Thom T. "Old Buck's going to be okay," he reported with satisfaction. "Doc Wagner says the vets in California were crazy as bedbugs to say he should be destroyed."

Thom T. nodded. "I seen horses hurt worse come back overnight. He's stiff and sore is all, but hell—so're you—and nobody offered to take *you* out and shoot you." The old blue eyes crinkled at the corners. "Well, except that one dude with the clipboard."

The smile they shared was comfortable and comforting. A rush of affection caught Trey by surprise. Buying the horse after it was written off by the movie company had been a generous impulse. Bringing Trey to Texas to recuperate, knowing full well that chances were about a million to one that he was the missing Taggart, was another.

But that was Thom T., Trey was beginning to realize; he liked to do nice things for people, preferably without fanfare. Maybe it wouldn't be so bad to be related to the old boy, after all. . . .

He stepped abruptly away from the buckskin with a final slap to the animal's neck. If he'd learned one thing in a rough-and-tumble life, it was that no amount of wishing could alter reality.

"So," he said brusquely, "that car I saw drive in a few minutes ago belongs to the lady librarian?"

"Yep. She's up to the house waitin' to meet you."

"Great." Trey grimaced. "She gonna do it?"

"Move in?" Thom T. led the way through the barn door, Trey falling into step. "Looks like it. Jesse worked on her this mornin' and I did the final arm-twistin' myself. She ain't too happy about it, but she couldn't think of a nice enough way to turn me down. Besides, the boy'll like it fine and she knows that."

"Okay. I've already thrown my stuff together and I can be out of the big house today if you'll give me the key to the little house."

"It ain't locked," Thom T. said in a pained voice. "Pickup truck okay?"

"Okay for what?"

"Okay for you to keep over there with you, what else? You need transportation, don't you?"

"I suppose, but—"

"But me no buts, boy. You can't be as slow as you're a-'actin. Keep that up and Rachel's gonna think you're a phony for sure, 'cause all us Taggarts 're playin' with a full deck."

The old man threw open the back door and stepped onto the glassed-in porch. "Rachel," he called, "here he is—Trey Smith, the lost sheep of the Taggart family. Or maybe I should make that the *black* sheep of the Taggart family. That suit you better, boy?"

He stepped aside, and Trey looked into the wide, hazel eyes of Showdown's lady librarian.

3

RACHEL HAD BEEN WAITING for Thom T. on the glass-enclosed porch, a frosty mug of lemonade in her hand and trepidation in her heart. What had she just let him talk her into?

She'd arrived with all her arguments at the ready and then realized she owed him far too much to turn him down, on this or any other request he might make of her.

Without Thom T. Taggart's support and influence, she'd still be "that trashy Cox girl—you know the youngest one with the baby that's got no *daddy.*" What she'd achieved had mostly been due to the old man's generosity; not for a minute did she believe that any standing she had in this town was due to anything other than Taggart patronage.

She wouldn't let him down—never. Nor would she put her own hard-won, still tenuous respectability in jeopardy. Lord knows, she'd paid for her mistakes and the price had been high, higher than she'd ever be able to pay again.

But sometimes...sometimes she just wanted to break loose. That was how she'd felt last night in the Alamo Cantina when the sexy Yankee with the devilish glint in his eyes had come on to her.

Who would know? she'd asked herself for one mad, mad moment. And then had come the inevitable answer: somebody would. She'd never been able to get away with anything.

So she was bowing to Thom T.'s wish. She'd move out here next week, but only on the clear understanding that she must return home before school started again.

It wouldn't be that bad, she encouraged herself. She might even be through within a week. How difficult could it be to organize a few reports and old documents? She enjoyed research; this should be a piece of cake.

That's right—a piece of cake.

A doorknob grated and she turned to see Thom T. stepping onto the porch. He was talking; she didn't hear what he was saying because of the other man. Rachel's heart slammed violently against the wall of her chest and she clamped her teeth to keep from betraying her shock. For there before her, a puzzled expression on his face, stood the damn Yankee who'd tried to pick her up last night at the Alamo.

THOM T.'S WATCHDOG didn't impress Trey. Hair slicked back over her ears, prim blue skirt, crisp white blouse and sensible walking shoes matched her unadorned face with its touch-me-not expression.

Yet he saw high color in her cheeks, heard a quaver in her voice when she said, "It's my understanding that we have yet to prove Mr. Smith's position in the family, Thom T."

Cool, Trey thought, icy, in fact. Her voice, cultured and precise, held just the barest hint of Southern softness, but she looked at him with obvious disapproval.

He felt his hackles rise. "I'm pleased to meet you, too," he said dryly, enjoying the quick flush of color his greeting brought to her cheeks.

If Thom T. sensed the tension, he didn't show it. "Knew you two'd take to each other like bees to clover," he announced.

"Or bears to honey," she agreed crisply. She hesitated for just an instant before offering her right hand. "How do you do, Mr. Smith? If you're who you say you are . . ."

Without thinking, Trey bore down upon the slender hand easily engulfed by his. "If I'm who *he* says I am."

Her eyes narrowed fractionally at the strength in his grip but she didn't try to pull away. "I stand corrected."

He released her hand and she turned toward the lemonade pitcher on a sideboard. Trey had the impression that she was shaken, stalling for time to compose herself. "So what's this so-called 'legend' you're all so worried about?" he demanded.

Thom T.'s glance went from one to the other, settling on her. "You tell him," he suggested.

She set down the pitcher. "Tell him what?"

"How it all begun."

"Which version?"

"The one everybody in the whole state of Texas believes in," the old man shot back. "Then I'll tell you both what *I* think."

She nodded. She knew the story so well that she could tell it even with those blue-gray eyes looking all the way through to her prevaricating soul.

She could tell it, even limp with relief that Trey Smith hadn't recognized her as Lizzie. It was vaguely insulting, and yet, how could he connect the mousy librarian with the red-hot mama from the Alamo Cantina?

Of course, he had no way of knowing that one persona was as false as the other. In a pinch one night, she'd actually fooled people she'd grown up with, so why not this Yankee stranger?

She took a deep breath and launched into the familiar tale. "They say that in 1876, Rose Taggart was the prettiest girl in three counties. She was certainly the belle of Jones, Texas, which was what they called Showdown in those days. She—"

"Got any pictures to back that up?"

Trey's question jarred her, breaking the flow of her recitation. "Well, yes, there are pictures, but—"

"Can I see one?"

Rachel tightened her lips; she just wanted to get this over with. "Really, Mr. Smith, I don't think—"

"Good idea," Thom T. interjected. "Come on into the parlor and we'll take us a look-see."

The old man led the way, Trey standing aside for Rachel to precede him. She felt the force of his gaze between her shoulder blades and resisted the urge to shiver.

Thom T. crossed the garnet-colored carpet to an antique wooden table against one parlor wall. Opening a leather-bound album, he selected a page, then offered it for their perusal.

A young, dark-haired woman stared directly at them from the photograph, her level gaze slightly challenging. An almost-smile hovered around her lips, as if she found her situation slightly ludicrous. Her dark, demure dress ended in a high collar with a froth of ruffles, out of which peeked a cameo brooch. She looked strong and smart and competent.

"There she is," Thom T. said with a smile. "Rose Taggart, my great-aunt and the woman who started it all. Your great-great-grandma, Trey."

"In your dreams," Trey shot back. He cocked his head to one side and stared at the photograph. "Southern belle, huh. Looks to me like she could raise a little hell herself."

"Looks can be deceiving," Rachel said. Realizing that applied to her more than it did to Rose, she continued her recital. "Rose was simply an innocent bystander. Do you want to hear this story or not?"

He grinned and the creases in his cheeks deepened. "I'm all ears."

She'd give him the condensed version, she decided, talk fast and get out of here. "Rose and the local sheriff were about to be married when a gunfighter known only as Boone rode into town. This Boone made advances to Rose—"

"Which she, as a 'decent' woman, no doubt repulsed."

Rachel lifted her chin and glared at him. "That's right. But being a thoroughly undesirable type, Boone tried to stop the wedding, anyway. There was a big shoot-out...."

"On Main Street at high noon?" He looked so amused, so superior. "When the gun smoke cleared, I suppose the belle of Jones, Texas, ended up with the winner."

"That's right," Thom T. chimed in. "She run off with the winner. And the winner just happened to be the gunfighter, not the sheriff."

"Thom T., no!" Rachel frowned. "That's impossible."

"How so?"

"W-well . . . for one thing, Boone the mysterious gunfighter was buried in the church graveyard in 1876."

"*Some*body's buried there."

His utter confidence was beginning to shake her. "Do you think Sheriff Jack's in that grave?"

"Nope. Jack Guthrie went back East alone. Turned up in Philadelphia, took up the practice of law like his daddy before him and married a Miss Ida Craven round about 1879."

Trey shook his head in candid disbelief. "Where do you people come up with this stuff, old cowboy movies?"

Rachel's palms itched to slap him. "No," she said coldly, "but our legend has been filmed several times, first as a silent movie along about 1925. Legend, Mr. Smith—a story that may or may not be true, handed down from the past. Everybody in Texas believes it's true, or did until recently."

She shot Thom T. a condemning glance. "Good grief, they wouldn't change the name of the town to commemorate something that didn't happen. Then there's Showdown Days to consider. . . ."

"You lost me," Trey said. "What's Showdown Days?"

Rachel kept her voice calm with an effort. "Showdown Days is a festival launched in 1947 to commemorate the legend. It lasts a full week and we even do historical reenactments. It attracts thousands of tourists to town every Fourth of July. It's incredibly important to the local economy."

She turned to Thom T. "There may be a few little niggling discrepancies between our legend and the truth, but the basic premise—"

"Is wrong. Dead wrong. I don't know *who* they buried under that marker but it ain't Boone Smith. That was his last name, Smith." Thom T. shot a meaningful glance at Trey.

Trey shrugged off that coincidence. "Him and who else? Not exactly a rare name, Smith."

"Hush," Rachel commanded. "Just hush for a minute, will you? This is no joking matter." She sat down hard on a green brocade chair. "But why did everybody in town join in the conspiracy?" she demanded of Thom T. "It doesn't make sense...."

Trey listened to them argue back and forth, but wasn't as interested in the veracity of an old story as he was in comparing this ice queen to the luscious Liz. Why he'd thought of the woman from the bar he couldn't say; perhaps something about Rachel reminded him of her.... But that was ludicrous! He laughed and saw Rachel glare at him.

They were both women; that was about all they had in common. Liz's masses of dark curly hair, worn free and wild, were a far cry from Rachel's slicked-back, old-maid twist. Liz dressed like a woman who liked to attract attention, Rachel like a born wallflower.

One was a good-time girl, the other a martyr. He damned sure knew the difference.

Rachel and Thom T. seemed to have reached an impasse about their disputed legend by the time the ringing of a telephone summoned the old man from the room. When Thom T. had gone, she leaned back in her chair with an air of total dejection.

She looked so absolutely crushed that Trey impulsively squatted beside her, leaning against the armrests and peering into her hazel eyes. She really wasn't as homely as he'd originally thought. In fact, with very little effort she'd be almost . . . attractive might not be too strong a word.

She stared at him as if he were about to bite her, leaning as far away as she could. Her uneasiness amused him, since his interest in martyrs was zilch.

"Cheer up," he commanded. "Since I seem to be the linchpin in Thom T.'s little fantasy, you haven't got a thing to worry about."

She blinked, long lashes brushing across high cheekbones. "I beg your pardon?"

"I'm not related to the Taggarts—hell, I'm not related to anybody. I guess what I'm saying is, don't let him tear up your legend to accommodate me."

"I . . . don't understand."

She forced the words past pale lips, and it dawned on him that she really *didn't* understand. Like everybody else, she thought he was up to no good.

Well, hell.

He stood and thrust his hands deep into the pockets of his shorts. "I get it," he said. "You think I'm working some kind of con here."

She shook her head. "I think you already *have*."

"What the hell's that supposed to mean?"

"Jesse told me about Thom T.'s will." She rose, too. "Tell Thom T. I had to go, will you? I'll be in touch."

Yeah, Trey thought, watching her hurry from the room. *Don't call me. I'll call you.*

"WHERE'S RACHEL?" Thom T. asked, looking around.

"She remembered a pressing engagement," Trey said

sarcastically. "Thom T., have you done anything stupid?"

The old guy reared back. "You mean lately or ever?"

"I mean lately, as you damn well know."

Thom T. refused to meet Trey's steady gaze. "Like what?"

"Oh, I don't know . . . Opened a million-dollar bank account in my name, written me into your will, something along those lines."

Thom T. brightened. "That about the bank account's a good idea. You need—?"

Trey groaned. Rachel had been right; he was in the will. "Take me out," he growled.

"Outa where?"

"Don't give me the innocent crap. I don't want or need your money, or anything else, for that matter."

"Nothin' at all? How about your rightful place in the family?"

The wistful tone cut like a laser but Trey hardened his heart. "Thom T., you're a cool old guy but you're pushing too hard," he warned. "I know where you stand and you know where I stand, so why don't you just back off and let the cards fall where they may?"

Thom T. sighed. "Rachel told you, huh? Jesse musta told her. That's what I get for runnin' off at the mouth."

"Who told who isn't the issue. Either I'm out of your will or I'm out of Texas. I'm beginning to think I never should have come in the first place."

"Sure, sure, whatever you say." Thom T. gave the younger man a soothing pat on the shoulder. "And while we're on the subject of blabbin', I'd appreciate it if you didn't say anything to anybody else about our legend bein' a crock of cow patties. If that got out it'd play hell with the locals. Why, it'd be like findin' out Columbus didn't discover America."

"Columbus *didn't* discover America, Thom T. Some Viking did."

The old man grinned. "Go on," he scoffed. "America's here, ain't it?"

Sharing a laugh, Trey was suddenly aware how much the old codger was getting to him. That wiped the smile off his face in a hurry. He had his own life to live, far from the confines of this dot on the Texas map.

His strength was growing everyday. Maybe it was time to think of leaving.

TREY MOVED into the foreman's house the same afternoon, over Thom T.'s protests.

"Rachel and her boy ain't comin' until next week, so what's your rush?" he railed.

Trey halted, his arms full of books and clothing. "Didn't you ever feel a need for privacy?" he demanded around a broad grin.

"You got privacy! Nobody around here but me'n' Elva, and she just cooks 'n' cleans and goes home. Only thing you could be a-needin' privacy for is—"

He stopped short and stared at Trey; a big grin creased the leathery face. "That Lizzie gal?"

Trey shrugged. "I could get lucky."

The old man sighed. "I know when I'm licked. Just you watch your tracks, boy. A woman can cause you a powerful heapa trouble, you not careful."

That was hardly news to Trey.

ABOUT SIX O'CLOCK, Trey finished putting away his possessions in his new bachelor pad and headed for town. Time to check out a few more of the local hot spots, maybe even get a line on Liz. He parked the pickup in the packed lot beside the Showdown Steak House and walked inside.

The place was crowded, waitresses literally running between the kitchen and the tables while balancing huge trays of steaming food atop their shoulders. Trey looked around, wondering if he'd even be able to get a table in this vinyl and wood grain paradise. The situation did not look promising until he spotted a vacant booth near the windows.

A waitress galloped up, grinning hugely. "Howdy. One for supper?"

"That's right."

Her grin slipped. Could she tell he was a stranger from only two words? "You'll have to wait," she announced, as if expecting him to argue.

"What about that booth over there?" He pointed with a quick thrust of his chin.

She shook her head vigorously. "Reserved."

"Really? Who for?"

"For me, I'm afraid."

A voice filled with humor came from behind him. Trey turned. A small, matronly woman of sixty or so smiled at him.

"I'm Dixie Baker." She offered her hand. "You'd be Thom T.'s houseguest."

Trey shook hands with her. "Trey Smith. How'd you know? Somebody pin a sign on my back that says Kick Me! I'm a Yankee?"

She shook her head. Her short, curly hair, pale as platinum was caught in the light coming through the windows behind her. "Word spreads fast in this town," she explained. To the waitress she added, "I'd be pleased to have Mr. Smith join me for supper, if he's a mind to."

He was. Hers was the first friendly face he'd seen since he hit town. He followed her zigzag path across the crowded room, aware of the suspicious glances darting his way, the respectful looks following her.

Dixie Baker nodded and spoke to everybody they passed, and they returned her greetings with a deference Trey didn't miss.

He slid onto a forest-green bench seat and reached for the paper napkin on the table. "So you know about me, huh?" He spread the napkin on his lap.

"No, Mr. Smith. Nobody in Showdown *knows* about you, as you put it. I ran into Thom T. yesterday at the post office and he told me you were some sort of distant relative who was visiting. He offered no further explanation nor did I seek one. I recognized you just now by his description and your accent, if that's what concerns you."

"What concerns me is you thinking I've got an accent," Trey admitted.

"When in Rome, Mr. Smith." Again that faint, slightly superior smile.

The waitress plunked down heavy, barrel-shaped glasses of water and two menus. "How's it goin' Miz Baker?" she asked respectfully.

"Very well, thank you, Claudene." Mrs. Baker put aside her unopened menu. "I'll have the usual, dear."

"Yes, ma'am." Claudene turned to Trey, pencil poised.

Trey looked at the woman across from him. "What's your usual?"

"The specialty of the house—chicken-fried steak with cream gravy. I'm not sure a . . ."

Trey laughed and threw down his menu. "You're either about to call me a Yankee or a damn Yankee, one or the other." He looked at Claudene. "Bring me what the lady's having."

"Right." Claudene scribbled on her pad. "Whatta you want to drink?"

"Lemonade in a dirty glass," Trey shot back.

"Say what?"

"Milk. A glass of milk will be fine."

Claudene walked away, muttering something under her breath that sounded like "foreigners." Trey settled back in his seat and looked at his dinner companion. She regarded him with a quizzical expression.

"What is it?" he asked.

"You ordered milk. It . . . reminded me of someone."

"Yeah? Who?" Trey picked up his glass of water and drank.

"My son." She said it very softly, then looked away quickly.

Trey hesitated. "I take it that's a difficult subject for you."

She nodded. "He died almost fourteen years ago. There's a certain quality about you that brings him to mind, Mr. Smith."

"Trey."

"Trey, then. And you may call me Dixie."

He arched one brow. "I'm not sure I should. I get the feeling that would be about like calling Queen Victoria 'Vickie.'"

That brought a real laugh from her. "That's the quality Bobby had, that irreverence. He had so much spirit! I wish..."

But whatever she was about to say was lost when a couple who had been dining nearby stopped to pay their respects on their way out. After that, it seemed no one was willing to leave the restaurant without first having a few words with the doyenne of Showdown society.

Trey watched curiously, noticing the way her manner changed depending upon who stood there. With some she was warm and friendly, with others cool but perfectly correct, and with one young man haughty and judgmental. She'd recently talked to his mother, she said, scolding him for unspecified peccadilloes.

But with each and every individual there remained no doubt that Dixie Baker was in charge. It was plain that she could make you or break you in this town with a wave of her hand.

Since Trey had no interest either in Showdown *or* its social strata, he felt perfectly comfortable asking, as they neared the conclusion of their meal, "So how'd you get to be queen bee around here?"

Dixie's eyes opened wide and she choked on a sip of coffee. Covering her mouth with her napkin, she coughed until the choking sounds turned into laughter. "I like you, Trey Smith," she said when she could talk again. "You're so very like my Bobby would have been had he lived."

"How old was he when he died?"

"Nineteen. His life was just beginning."

"Accident?"

She nodded. "He quarreled with his father about a girl. Neither of them wanted me to know the details, but a few days later Bobby joined the army. He was killed in a training accident only a few months later . . . and it almost killed his father when we got the news."

When she spoke of her son, her whole manner changed. It occurred to Trey that people who knew her probably avoided the subject even now, out of respect for her loss. "Was he married?"

"No, sadly."

"Any children?"

"Really, Mr.—Trey. I'd give anything to have a grandchild, but I told you Bobby wasn't married."

He gave her his best crooked grin. "Really, Mrs.—Dixie, one doesn't depend on the other."

For a moment he thought he'd gone too far; then she laughed ruefully. "You're right, of course. That must have sounded pompous."

"Sure as hell did, Dixie." Trey swiped up the last bite of steak in the gravy. "Why do people tippy-toe around you the way they do?"

She shrugged. "Habit, I suppose. My late husband Cleve owned the local bank. He was . . . an older gentleman, and somewhat imposing. Some might have said intimidating."

"Scared everybody to death, did he?"

"Just about. People are creatures of habit, Trey. Once they make up their minds it's hard to get them to consider an alternate opinion." She cocked her head to one side. "I suppose that's why I dine alone each Saturday night at the Showdown Steak House."

Trey shook his head. "I still don't get it."

"I'm an institution," she said. "Nobody feels comfortable with an institution, now do they?"

Her hand lay beside her plate. On an impulse, he picked it up and raised it gallantly to his lips. "I do, Dixie Baker. How about you and me going honky-tonkin' some night soon?"

She giggled; she actually giggled. Trey knew people were beginning to stare, but she took no notice. "I'd like that," she said. "Believe it or not, I really would."

"Then count on it." He slid to the edge of his seat and stood up, pulling his wallet from the hip pocket of his shorts.

"Put your money away, Trey."

"No chance." He pulled out a handful of bills.

"Your money's no good here. Put it away, if you please."

Something in her tone told him she wasn't kidding. He stopped fumbling with the bills and looked at her. Her expression was warm and friendly.

"Thank you," she said, her voice rich with sincerity. "I didn't think you were the type of young man whose masculinity would be threatened if a woman bought him his supper. And I want to. This has been a delightful diversion for me. If I can ever be of assistance to you...."

"Maybe you can." He slid his wallet back into his pocket. "Ever hear of a girl called Liz or Lizzie? Young, good-looking, sexy?"

Dixie considered. "I can't think of any such person in Showdown. There's Lizzie Goodfellow, of course, but she's even older than I am."

Trey felt a shaft of disappointment, but that wasn't his only lead. "Okay, how about a kid named Laddy Cox?"

He saw instantly that he'd hit pay dirt. Her expression changed, grew guarded. "I know the Coxes."

"Can you tell me where they live?"

"Certainly. Go south on Main Street until you get to the little white church on the hill. Turn right one block. It's the small gray bungalow on the corner, on a big lot with lots of trees and swings hanging in back."

He grinned and winked at her. "Thanks. That's all I needed to know." He turned away, then hesitated. "Thanks for dinner," he said. "You're quite a babe."

He heard her laugh as he walked through the restaurant, not caring whether the other diners were watching.

HE FOUND the Cox house easily. Pulling up beneath the branches of a big old pecan tree, he looked the place over. Small, but neat and clean. Someone had put in a lot of work on the old house. Seemed unlikely it was Laddy.

Trey climbed out of the pickup and started up the walkway. The front screen door slammed open and a boy of twelve or thirteen ambled out, a half-eaten apple in one hand and an open book in the other. Engrossed in the story, he plowed into Trey on the steps.

Trey caught the boy's elbows to keep him from falling. "Watch it, kid," he suggested mildly.

The boy's glasses had fallen off one ear and hung haphazardly across his face. He righted them, at the same time trying to shove the book beneath his arm. "I'm sorry," he said. "I didn't see you."

"No problem." Trey hesitated. "I'm looking for Laddy Cox."

"He's inside."

"Thanks, kid." On a whim Trey added, "You wouldn't know a woman called Liz, would you?"

"Sure. My mother—that's her nickname. But hardly anyone calls her that except my Uncle Laddy."

There was something wrong here; the Liz he sought hadn't looked old enough to have a kid this big. "Can you tell me where I can find her?"

"Sure. She's inside, too." The boy cupped his mouth with one hand and bellowed, "Ma! Someone to see you!"

"Thanks, kid," Trey said dryly.

"My name's Jason."

"Then thanks, Jason." Trey bounded up the rest of the steps and across the small porch. He was vaguely aware that the boy stood on the walkway watching for a moment before lifting his book to reading level and walking on.

Trey wasn't thinking about the boy, or Laddy Cox, or even Dixie Baker. *Liz!* She was going to have some serious explaining to do when he—

The screen door swung open and there stood Rachel the librarian. "Yes?" she said coolly; then her long-lashed eyes went wide and she added, "You! What in the world are *you* doing here?"

Trey wanted to ask her the same question.

4

TREY OPENED HIS MOUTH, just as the truth clobbered him: Rachel *was* Liz. Could Laddy Cox, the kid Jason's "Uncle Laddy," be her brother?

Suddenly aware his mouth was hanging open, he snapped it shut. "Damn," he said softly. "Damn!"

What the hell was going on here? Rachel was older than Liz and plain instead of gorgeous. Rachel was shorter, her hair was not as dark . . . and her figure . . . He ran his befuddled gaze down the length of the woman standing staunchly in the doorway. Rachel's figure, what he could see of it beneath the generic librarian's outfit, was nothing special.

The woman stiffened before his perusal, her cheeks turning pink. "Did you come here just to swear at me?" she inquired in the chilly voice he'd heard before, "or is there something else you wanted?"

"I . . ." Trey thought fast. The voice and accent were different, and so were the expression and posture. Everything was different.

Except the nickname. And the connection to Laddy Cox, who, new insight told Trey, had treated the lovely Liz exactly as a younger brother might be expected to treat a disapproving older sister.

Trey tried again. "I . . . we've got to talk." *Lame, real lame.* He'd have to do better than that.

Rachel frowned. "We spoke only a few hours ago," she pointed out with the kind of patience she might use on an unreasonable library patron.

"Yes, but if we're going to work together . . ."

"*Work* together? I hardly think that's part of the bargain." She arched one dark brow, looking extremely skeptical.

"Yeah, well that's one of the things we need to talk about." He looked past her pointedly, into the living room. "Don't you want to invite me in?"

"No, Mr. Smith, I do not wish to invite you in. You may say what you came to say right here." She tightened her grip on the open screen door and stared back at him, her face expressionless.

Ice cold. She couldn't possibly be that hot little number from the Alamo. A new possibility occurred to him and he inquired hopefully, "You wouldn't have a sister would you?"

She let out her breath in an exasperated rush. "I don't think that's any of your business. If that's all . . ."

She started to close the screen door, her gesture dismissing him. Trey stuck out one foot to wedge the screen partially open. "That's not all, not nearly damn all." *Calm down, Smith—don't blow it. If this really is Liz, you sure as hell don't want her to know you're wise to her—until the time is ripe.* A sudden inspiration made him add, "I told Thom T. to take me out of the will."

She stepped back, letting her hand fall from the screen door. He immediately took advantage and pushed inside. The front door opened directly into the living room, with no hallway of any kind.

Her cool seemed about to desert her. She licked her lips; the pale lips he'd noted earlier, not like Liz's bright mouth. But full and soft, when not tight with disapproval.

Trey gave her his hopeful smile. "I sure could use something cold to drink. Then we can talk this over."

She was shaking her head before he got the words out of his mouth. "There's nothing to talk over. I should never have mentioned a will."

"Why not? You're entitled to your opinion, and in your opinion I'm a fake."

"I never called you a fake!"

"Not even to yourself?"

She looked affronted. "What I say to myself is my own business."

He nodded in ready agreement. "But what if *I* say I'm a fake? Does that give us something to talk about?"

She frowned. He'd obviously confused her and he savored that advantage. "Rachel, the world is full of fakes," he added. *And you know what I'm talking about, lady.* "Damn few people are what they seem to be." *Including you.* "We're all fakes in one way or the other." *Yeah, for example, a prissy librarian dressing up like a cowgirl-cutie to prowl local hot spots.*

"That's . . ." she swallowed hard and refused to meet his gaze ". . . an interesting theory. Perhaps we should have a little talk after all."

Turning, she indicated that he should take a seat on the couch. For a moment he saw her in profile: the classically straight nose, the clean line of forehead and chin, the sexy curve of full lips. Hazel eyes flashed defensively before she lowered her lids, dark lashes fanning out against her smooth, olive skin.

The sure and certain knowledge of her identity landed like a rock in the pit of his stomach. He'd bet dollars to donuts that Rachel's middle name was Elizabeth.

But why the disguise? What was she afraid of? Until he had a few answers, he'd keep his own counsel.

RACHEL LEANED against the kitchen sink, trying to catch her breath. Damn Trey Smith, damn the man for coming here! He'd caught her completely off guard. At first she'd been sure he'd seen through her little charade, but that awful moment had passed, now she was equally sure that he hadn't.

No, of course he wouldn't connect the dull librarian with the high-flying Liz, she comforted herself while she poured sun tea over ice cubes. Placing both glasses on a cork-lined tray, she added spoons and sugar; after a moment's hesitation, she opened a cookie jar shaped like an apple and piled the last of the fig bars on a small plate.

Carrying the tray into the living room, she told herself that the worst was undoubtedly over. If he was going to connect her with her alter ego, he'd have done so already. She was safe; of course she was.

Anyway, in all likelihood she'd never have to see him again after today. Hadn't he just admitted he was a fake? Whatever had made him come clean, he would doubtless slink back beneath whatever rock he'd been hiding under when Thom T. found him.

Not a minute too soon. There was something about Trey Smith that brought out the worst in Rachel Elizabeth Cox. Just being in the same room with him seemed to heat her blood and send chills racing up and down her spine, all at the same time. This she didn't need.

Not that having him around would jeopardize her hard-won self-control. She wouldn't let it. To prove it, she set the tray upon the coffee table, straightened and deliberately looked him full in the face.

And wished she hadn't when her mouth went dry and her heart started to pound. Because say what she would to comfort herself, the fact remained that Trey Smith was the sexiest man she'd ever laid eyes on. She'd thought so last night in the Alamo and again this afternoon at the Rocking T; she knew so here, in her own small living room. Even the bluish bruises on his forehead and high cheekbones didn't diminish his appeal.

But the danger seemed so much greater now that he'd intruded on her private space. Home was a refuge, a place where she didn't need to guard every word and thought. Until now, anyway; until Trey Smith had barged in.

He took a tall glass from the tray and drank as if he never expected to get another chance. He set the glass down to the frosty tinkle of ice cubes.

"Thanks," he said, his mouth curving up in a slight smile that could be teasing. "I needed that."

Rachel refused to be drawn into social chitchat. She added two spoonfuls of sugar to her own glass, gave the contents a perfunctory stir, and moved to the chair across from Trey Smith.

Sitting down, she placed her glass upon the lamp table and faced him with firm resolve. "All right, Mr. Smith, you said—"

"Call me Trey."

She frowned. She preferred to call him nothing. "You told me you're a fake. Would you care to explain?"

"I may have overstated the situation."

"I'm sorry, I don't understand."

"I'm not a fake . . . exactly."

Rachel felt the knot in the pit of her stomach tightening again. "Then do you maintain that you are indeed the long-lost descendant of Rose Taggart?"

"I'm not maintaining anything of the kind."

She sighed in exasperation. "Then perhaps you'd better tell me exactly what it is you *did* mean."

"Sure." He sprawled back on the couch, his long, strong legs in khaki-colored shorts extended beneath the table. He wore multicolored athletic shoes with red socks, and an aqua-blue T-shirt exhorting all within eyesight to give to the Los Angeles Symphony.

"The thing is," he began slowly, choosing his words with obvious care, "that old guy came to me. I didn't go to him. *He* thinks I'm his long-lost whatever, and I think he's Loony Tunes. I told him so. I told him there wasn't a chance in hell that I was his man."

"Why not, Mr. —?"

"Trey."

"Whatever."

"Because I'm an orphan."

That would gain him no sympathy from her . . . if she could help it. "All that means is that you don't *know* who your forebears were. You had them, just the same."

His jaw, firm even in repose, set at a stubborn angle. He had a slight cleft in his chin, and lines like parentheses on each side of an incredibly sensual mouth. *She had to stop thinking such things!* She looked at her hands, clasped in her lap, knuckles white.

"Maybe so," Trey conceded morosely. He leaned forward and picked up a cookie. "But I grew up in New York City and I have no reason to believe I ever lived anywhere else."

"Where did Thom T. find you?"

He looked the fig bar over, then popped it into his mouth. "California," he mumbled. "San Diego, actually. He came to the set—"

"A film set?"

"Yeah."

"You're in movies?"

He raised one dark brow. "Not the way you obviously mean." He picked up the small plate of cookies and balanced it on one long, muscular thigh. "I'm not an actor."

"Then what do you do?"

He thought about that for a moment. "I guess you could say I do whatever the big shots aren't up for."

"I see." He was some kind of gofer, perhaps a roustabout. Not a big-money job, certainly. A rich old man determined to befriend him could have looked like a heaven-sent opportunity. "So to return to the point, if you don't think you're related to Thom T., why did you come back to Texas with him?

"That's a good question." He shoved one hand through his unruly black hair. "I'd been in an accident and I was pretty banged up."

She nodded, remembering his words last night: "Horse threw me." She saw his eyes suddenly narrow to slits as if he were privy to her thoughts, so she added quickly, "I noticed the stitches above your eyebrow, and you limp a little once in a while."

"Yeah. Anyway, I needed a place to recuperate, and the old guy was pressuring me, so I told him I'd come along for the ride. But I didn't promise him a damned thing and I don't want a damned thing from him." He shrugged. "Except what he offered—a place away from the rat race where I can get myself into shape again."

Get into shape? She stared in disbelief. The man was a veritable mass of rippling muscle and glowing health.

He replaced the empty cookie dish on the coffee table and stood up, carefully uncoiling his tall frame. He started to speak, but his gaze went past her, fastening on something behind her. "And you," he added softly, "can believe it or not, because I simply do not give a flying—"

Rachel stiffened, knowing before she turned what she'd see.

Trey stifled a grin as he watched the kid walk into the room, strutting and pawing like a young bull. A plaid shirt trailed from one hand; he fixed a baleful glare upon Trey as if he'd invaded private turf.

Trey had been young once himself, about a thousand years ago. He understood young Laddy Cox and didn't fault him for being possessive. This was his home and his sister. A man protected what was his.

If anything was.

The boy halted in the middle of the room to shrug into the shirt. Without buttoning it, he shoved the tails into the waistband of his Levi's, glaring all the while. His lips curled back over white teeth. "Damned cat's up in that tree outside my window again," he announced to Rachel. "If I had a BB gun or a .22, I swear I'd—"

"Laddy! We have company."

She was nervous again; Trey heard it in her tight voice and saw it in the anxious glance she darted his way. She *should* be nervous, he thought with satisfaction. That kid could very easily blow her little masquerade right out of the water.

Time to take matters into his own hands. "We've met," he said in a flat, unfriendly voice. "Sort of."

"We have?" Laddy frowned. "Can't say I recall...." His eyes went wide. Long-lashed hazel eyes. Hazel eyes like Rachel's.

Hazel eyes like Liz's.

Trey nodded. "You got it—last night at the Alamo. You kinda started a riot, then took off and left the rest of us to work things out."

"I remember you!" Laddy's eyes grew bright. "You came with—" He darted a quick glance at Rachel.

"Within an inch of spending the night in a cage," Trey inserted smoothly. "Man, I was just an innocent bystander until you showed up and started World War III."

"What's the matter, can't handle yourself?" Laddy inquired with a sneer. "You damn Yankees are all alike. You come down here and—"

"Laddy!" Rachel jumped to her feet and grabbed his arm, much as she had last night in the cantina. "Shut up for just a minute, will you?"

Her tone brooked no further nonsense and Laddy subsided, mumbling under his breath. With a sigh that could only be relief, Rachel made the introductions. "Trey Smith, this is my brother Laddy Cox. Laddy, Trey is—" she hesitated "—a guest at the Rocking T."

"Huh?" Laddy frowned at his sister. "What's a damn Yankee—?"

"That tears it." Trey stood up, clenching hands into fists at his sides. "The next person who calls me a damn Yankee had better be prepared to back it up."

"Laddy! Laddy!" A new and very young voice, frantic with worry, interrupted. All three swung toward the door in instant response. A little girl of perhaps five stood there, tears streaming down her face; wringing her hands and shifting her weight from one foot to the other.

Rachel hurried to kneel beside the child. "What is it, Debbie Sue?" She brushed at the tear tracks on the dusty cheeks. "Don't cry, honey. Just tell us what's wrong and we'll help you, I promise."

"It's . . ." She struggled valiantly with her sobs. "It's Fluffy! He's stuck again!"

Laddy groaned. "Yeah, I heard him. Debbie Sue, how many times do I have to tell you that cat can get down out of a tree all by—?"

"No, Laddy, this time he really is stuck! He's at the very top and he's *afraid!* You've got to save him, Laddy! Please?"

Laddy shook his head decisively, and Trey's opinion of the boy dropped another couple of notches. Jeez, what kind of guy wouldn't rescue a child's kitten from a tree? How much trouble could that be?

Obviously too much for Laddy. "Debbie Sue Greenleaf, how many cat skeletons you ever see in a tree? When he gets hungry, he'll come on down."

"But Fluffy...but Fluffy..." Debbie burst into a fresh torrent of tears.

Rachel gathered the sobbing child into her arms, giving her brother a reproachful glance across the girl's heaving shoulders. "Laddy, don't you think that just this once more you could?"

"No, I don't. I've hauled that damned cat outa that tree for the last time."

Debbie turned her tear-stained face toward Trey, as if in a last resort. "Mister," she cried in a voice that could have melted steel, "please save my kitty!"

WELL, WHAT COULD HE DO? Standing at the foot of a towering oak tree, Trey gazed up through the leafy branches, trying to catch a glimpse of Fluffy, completely hidden by foliage but meowing piteously and at the top of its lungs.

It wasn't as if he'd *volunteered* for this job, Trey reminded himself; the little girl had turned those teary blue eyes on him and he hadn't had much choice. But what the hell— It was no big deal to climb a tree and rescue one small, helpless bundle of fur. All in a day's work.

After all, he was a professional.

RACHEL WATCHED as Trey mentally measured the distance from the ground to the first branch. She knew she should warn him.

She really should warn him. On the other hand, he could stand being taken down a peg or two.

Bending, he sprang into the air and grabbed a thick branch, then swung himself up. In little more than the flash of an eye he was sitting there, looking up to find his next handhold. He looked exceedingly confident and in complete control.

But when he stood, she saw that he favored one leg. What if it gave out on him? What if he fell or otherwise hurt himself?

She squeezed Debbie Sue's hand tighter. What if he made it all the way to the top before realizing he was trying to rescue a saber-toothed tiger?

In the name of common decency she must warn him, even if his cocky self-confidence did set her teeth on edge. "Trey!" she called. "I think there's something you should— Mmm!"

Laddy's fingers clamped over her mouth, cutting off the warning, and Trey swung up the next level. By the time he was settled and could respond to her unfinished communication, Laddy had released his hold on her.

"Did you say something?" Trey called from his perch a good twenty-five or thirty feet above the ground.

"Well, I—I wanted to wish you good luck!"

"Yeah, mister," Debbie chimed in. "Good luck!"

He gave them a cheery wave and climbed higher, passing out of sight behind the leafy curtain. They measured his progress by the rustling of leaves and creaking of tree limbs, occasionally punctuated by a swear word. Higher and higher he climbed, to the accompaniment of the feline's bloodcurdling wails, and then . . .

Intense silence descended so suddenly that Rachel stopped breathing. Even Debbie Sue stood still to stare up in awe. Laddy tilted his head and his satisfied grin grew wider.

"*Damnation!*" Trey's howl of disbelief apparently shook loose old Fluffy, who let out a wildcat roar. Leaves rustled against each other as if struck by gale force winds, limbs shook, the giant tree itself seemed to quiver. Horrified, Rachel saw in her mind's eye Trey and the big black alley cat come face-to-face, before the furry feline launched itself through space to dig razor-sharp claws into its unsuspecting and unprepared rescuer....

What have I done? she wondered in panic, listening while the thrashing sounds grew louder and came closer. That damned cat; he was nothing but trouble, the whole neighborhood said so. Only Debbie Sue loved him, and so he'd been allowed to hang around, causing trouble.

A horrible cracking sound warned her that the old oak was not standing up well to such abuse. Laddy grabbed her around the waist and she hung on to Debbie while he hauled them back to safety.

"Look out!" he shouted. "A limb's coming down!"

Rachel prayed. She clutched Debbie Sue, closed her eyes and prayed, *"Please don't let him break his neck in my tree. Thom T. would never understand."*

A broken branch plummeted to earth with a thud. In the same instant Debbie pulled free. "Fluffy!" she shouted, taking off at a run after the furry black streak heading west at approximately the speed of sound. "Come back, Fluffy! I want to hug you!"

Rachel was afraid to look at the tree, terrified of what she might see. Would Trey Smith be crushed beneath the huge tree limb? Had he fallen all the way to the ground or was he still . . . ?

Laddy began to laugh. Rachel whirled, perfectly prepared to rip her brother's heart out, but what she saw instead was Trey Smith.

Trey Smith, dangling by one arm from a branch a good thirty feet in the air. Trey Smith, bloody streaks marking the side of his face where Fluffy had clawed him. Trey Smith, his California T-shirt in bloody shreds.

Trey Smith, looking down at them and laughing maniacally. Then, before her astonished gaze, he swung his body out, released his hold on that limb and dropped like a stone to catch a lower branch.

Tarzan couldn't have descended with greater speed and grace.

And Jane couldn't have been more impressed, even later while pouring alcohol over assorted scrapes and cuts left by that accursed cat and an unforgiving tree. Trey didn't make a sound, just sat there stoically as if it didn't hurt at all.

Even Laddy seemed a bit awed. "How d' you learn to do that, drop limb to limb without breaking your neck?" he demanded.

"Did I do that?" Trey's eyes widened in mock surprise. "I must have been in such a hurry to get away from Fluffy that I didn't know what I was doing."

"Yeah, right," Laddy agreed sarcastically. He cocked his head to one side. "You mad? About Fluffy, I mean."

Trey stood up and reached for his shredded shirt. Rachel tried not to stare at his bare chest with its mat of curling black hair, but found herself doing so nonetheless. Weak. She was too damned weak.

"Nah, I'm not mad." Trey pulled the ragged knit over his head and dragged it over his washboard-rippled middle. "About Fluffy, anyway. I'm none too happy about what happened last night, though."

She saw Laddy's cheeks flush. "Look, man, you were just in the wrong place at the right time. You never heard of a fight in a bar? If you can't take it, go back where you come from."

Trey heard him out stoically. "Kid," he said in a soft, menacing voice, "where I come from we chew up little boys like you and spit 'em out. You showed up drunk and stupid last night, started a brawl and then went sneaking out the back door. You tell me who can't take it."

He walked to the door and paused with his hand on the latch. "I don't like drunks and I don't like druggies," he said, his lip curling. "They don't care who they hurt. When they go, they have an unfortunate tendency to take some innocent SOB with them. I decided a long time ago it wouldn't be me—it sure as hell wouldn't be me."

It sounded almost like a prophecy, and Rachel felt sick with fear that he might be right. There was no way she could defend Laddy's actions last night. Or her own. Nor could she apologize, as she longed to do; she wasn't even supposed to know what had happened, at least not firsthand.

"Wait!" she cried. "I . . . you . . ." It would help if he wouldn't just stand there, looking at her so expectantly. "I . . . I'm sorry you were hurt, by the cat, I mean. I feel responsible. . . ."

He looked disappointed, as if he'd expected something more. "Don't, because you're not. We're all responsible for our own actions, dumb though they may be."

The cold, blue-gray gaze slashed at Laddy, who glared back. But Rachel wasn't concerned with her brother at that moment. The more Trey excused her, the guiltier she felt.

"I should have warned you about Fluffy," she said. "At least let me drive you over to see Dr. Preston. I don't think stitches are necessary, but you might need a tetanus shot or something."

The blood literally rushed from Trey's face. He looked afraid . . . ?

But that was ridiculous. This man had climbed to the top of one of the tallest trees in Showdown, wrestled with a wild cat, ridden down on a falling branch, saved himself from more serious injury—perhaps even death—by catching another limb as he plummeted past.

This was not a man who'd blanch at the mention of a tetanus shot, for heaven's sake!

But he had, try though he might to conceal that fact. She watched him try, then shake his head, spin around and disappear through the front doorway.

Behind her she heard Laddy mutter, "Chicken! Scared of a little shot."

TREY GRIPPED the steering wheel and shuddered. He never knew what would trigger the memories. Sometimes, like now, even the word "shot" had the power to bring it all rushing back to him. . . .

An overwhelming sense of helplessness crushed him, the same helplessness he'd felt that long-ago day in the alley when they'd pinned him down and bared his arm. He'd relived it many times: young faces of many colors leering at him, the needle moving closer and closer, growing bigger and more threatening. . . .

Twisting, turning, fighting for his life . . . his gut, his whole body clenched in anticipation of the jolt. A stabbing pain, a voice: "Hold him still, goddammit! I gotta find a vein." Cold steel violating warm flesh again and again; finally a grunt of satisfaction from his tormentors and the grasping, punishing hands fell away.

Alley smells of rotting garbage and smoke choked him; he heard the distant wail of a siren and the thunder of running feet but couldn't move, couldn't breathe. Sweat broke out on his forehead; he had to move or he was dead. . . .

Passing a trembling hand across his eyes, Trey straightened behind the wheel of Thom T.'s pickup and sucked in a deep breath of clean air. That was another life in another place, he reminded himself. He'd been a smart-assed seventeen-year-old, but he'd survived the hit—barely. Others he knew and loved hadn't been so lucky. . . if you could call anyone growing up in that environment lucky.

Needles meant drugs and drugs meant death, whether in a hospital or on the streets. He knew his phobia was unreasonable, but there didn't seem to be a hell of a lot he could do about it.

Except refuse to think about it. He'd think about something else.

He'd think about Rachel, he decided, pulling away from the curb.

And Liz—he'd think about her, too. With pleasure.

5

TREY SMITH leaned against the counter of the Showdown Public Library, his expression bland but his eyes full of the devil. "Where can I find *The Joy of Sex?*" he inquired.

Rachel's sense of humor got the better of her. "In this town, Mr. Smith, you probably can't." When he chuckled, she widened her eyes in mock astonishment. "Oh, you mean the *book?* Through that door and to your right."

He made no move to follow her directions. "I doubt I can find it without help. I'm a stranger here, you know."

She glanced significantly at him, taking in the neon-pink biking shorts and black T-shirt, the biking helmet and gloves shoved under one arm. The shorts left nothing to the imagination.

Nothing.

She didn't know where he'd got the bike, but he'd pedaled up to the library steps before she'd even gotten the door unlocked. Obviously his recent brush with Fluffy hadn't done him any long-lasting harm.

His unexpected presence in her library was doing Rachel harm, however. Every time she looked up she found herself staring at his high, tight buns, or some other interesting portion of his anatomy.

She turned to the page stacking books on a cart. "Marcy, please show Mr. Smith where the how-to sex manuals are located," she requested sweetly.

"You bet." Butter wouldn't melt in Marcy's mouth, but as she passed Rachel the girl muttered in an aside, "And I'll let him practice on me, if he wants to."

Rachel watched them disappear out of sight, then turned back to the counter. Steve Summers stood there with a book and a hopeful expression. She hadn't even seen him come in, which made her frown in irritation at Trey and his distractions.

She picked up Steven's book: *Insurance from A to B.* It figured. Steve lived, ate and sold insurance.

He smiled, dipping his chin with a shyness inexplicable in a forty-some-year-old man, especially an insurance salesman. "You're looking very well, Rachel," he said. "How's Jason?"

"He's fine." She couldn't help comparing Steve to Trey, the guy with the self-assured smile and jaunty athlete's body. Steve was at least six inches shorter and many pounds lighter; in fact, he reminded her of Woody Allen. She and Steve had gone out a few times over the years, and although his conversations ran heavily toward the boring—insurance, for example— she'd been grateful for the male companionship.

Rachel knew she scared men off, especially men aware of her past who tended to think of her in terms of a quick and easy score. Instead, they soon found themselves brushing figurative egg off their faces. A tarnished reputation was a hard thing to polish up again, and she'd stepped on innumerable male egos doing so.

Since her own hopes and expectations always seemed at odds with those of the men in this town, she'd all but stopped dating. Until Trey came along, she'd thought she was resigned to her manless fate. No, damn it, she *was* resigned!

She stamped the return date inside the book and slid it across the counter to Steve. "Hope you like it."

"I do. I've read it twice already." He gave her a tentative smile. "Uhh . . . Rachel, I don't know if you've heard but my father's finally retiring. I'm throwing a big farewell party Friday for him and my mother before they leave on an around-the-world cruise."

Over his shoulder she saw Trey appear in the doorway, a thick volume in his hand and a challenging light in his eyes. He glanced at Steve and raised one brow.

Impulsively she leaned across the counter and hastily said a single word: "Yes."

Steve blinked owlishly. "Yes?"

"You're inviting me to your parents' party, right? My answer is yes. I wouldn't miss it for the world."

"That's great," he said enthusiastically. "I wasn't sure how you'd feel about goin' to the Yellow Rose. I'll pick you up Friday night at seven. This is gonna be fun!"

TREY COULD HAVE telephoned Dixie but decided to pedal over to her house instead, perversely enjoying the stares and minor commotions his attire created along the way. Dropping the bike against the broad front steps of her old Victorian mansion, he bounded up and pounded on the door.

She answered almost immediately, frowning until she saw who it was. She took in his appearance and laughed. "My word, that's some outfit," she allowed.

"Would you care to come inside where the neighbors can't see you?"

He grinned. "What they see is what they get. But I didn't drop by just to shock the neighbors."

"Although you do enjoy doing that," she suggested.

"As long as it's no particular effort."

Dixie stepped aside and gestured to him to enter. "Then why are you here?"

"I'm looking for a date." He pulled off his helmet as he walked past her. "Remember when I said I'd take you honky-tonkin' one of these days? How does the Yellow Rose Friday night sound?"

TREY ELBOWED HIS WAY past the batwing doors and into the Yellow Rose, Dixie Baker on his arm. It was shortly after eight Friday night and the party was in full swing. Apparently Steve had reserved the entire establishment for festivities to provide a proper parental send-off, festivities to which Dixie had been invited. She hadn't planned to attend, however, until Trey made her an offer she declared she couldn't refuse.

To Trey, the Yellow Rose looked like the set of a Western movie, except everything was on a smaller, more realistic scale. Even the people looked like movie extras, the men wearing boots and jeans and bright shirts, the women in everything from glittering cocktail dresses to double knits.

A three-piece Western band on the stage opposite the long, mahogany bar sawed out a Texas two-step for couples hopping, skipping and jumping around the dance floor. Trey felt unaccountably pleased to be part of the affair, even if he was more or less a carpetbagger.

Lingering near the entry to absorb his surroundings, a feeling of permanence stole over him. How many generations of Taggarts had stood where he stood now? He shivered. Gunfighters, cowboys, even soiled doves had passed this way.

Dixie, watching with an approving smile, nodded. "Wonderful, isn't it? The oldest parts of this building date back to the eighteen-seventies. It's been restored as closely to the original as possible, since it's an important part of Showdown Days every year."

Showdown Days. That was the celebration Rachel and Thom T. were so eager to protect, Trey remembered. Its future depended on the love life of Thom T.'s great-something-or-other, Rose Taggart. Strange, he mused, how often history turned on a woman's choice of bedmate.

The secret was safe with him. He wasn't a Taggart, he was a Smith, what-the-hell-ever that might mean.

But what if the gunfighter, Boone Smith, really was Trey's great-great-grandfather? He grinned; he didn't have all that much trouble seeing himself related to a gunfighter.

But Rose Taggart as his great-great-grandmother? Not a chance. Regardless of Thom T.'s opinion, Rose must have married the sheriff. Why would a Southern belle get involved with a gun-slinging outsider? Better still, why would that kind of man want such a woman?

Turning toward Dixie, he caught an unexpected glimpse of Rachel on the dance floor and stopped short. *Where in the hell had she found a dress that ugly?* he wondered, taking in the loose-to-the-point-of-shapeless brown garment. And those shoes, clunky and unattractive and downright silly paired with such slim and shapely ankles—ankles shown to advantage as she danced with Steve. She moved with grace and unexpected confidence, obviously having a wonderful time.

Her hair was still pinned back, not loose and curly and sexy the way Trey knew it could be. But despite her efforts, she couldn't completely conceal that other side of herself. Wild tendrils escaped the bun to swirl around her flushed cheeks, and her face glowed with a zest he'd never seen there before.

Her normal reserve just didn't seem to be holding up very well. All Liz's latent sensuality was right there beneath Rachel's surface, waiting to explode. And by God, it was going to explode for him, he promised himself.

The good-time girl was part martyr, and vice versa; that duality intrigued the hell out of him. Had that been Rose Taggart's appeal, as well? Perhaps she had been more than the simple Southern beauty of history and legend. Another shiver rippled down Trey's spine and he felt his scalp tighten. *If Boone Smith was anything like me, and Rose Taggart was anything like Rachel . . .*

Still on the dance floor, Rachel turned abruptly and her glance collided with Trey's. She stood stock-still. Steve, clutching one of her hands, danced around her with abandon, but she ignored his gyrations.

Dammit, this was scary. All Trey wanted to do was sleep with her, he didn't want to get personal. *What had Boone wanted from Rose? What had he got?*

Trey took Dixie's elbow in a grip so severe that she flinched and gave him a look of surprised disapproval. "Let's belly up to the bar, ma'am," he invited, hustling her in that direction.

Anything to short-circuit that electrical connection.

RACHEL WASN'T having fun anymore.

Trey stood out in this cowboy crowd like a coyote in a henhouse. In his white pleated trousers and matching, full-sleeved shirt, he looked as if he belonged beneath a slow-moving ceiling fan in Casablanca, not in the middle of a good ol' Texas hoedown.

He also looked . . . wonderful, all dark and dangerous and sexy. Then Rachel saw the woman on his arm and stopped breathing.

If there was one person in town she sought to avoid, it was Dixie Baker, her son's grandmother.

Not that Dixie knew that, or ever would. . . .

THE FIRST TIME Bobby Baker noticed her, Rachel was sitting on the bridge over Cayuse Creek, wondering whether she should just jump in and end her misery. Earlier that day she'd overheard several girls whispering behind the gym lockers about her sister Naomi.

"She must have slept with every guy in Showdown between the ages of sixteen and sixty," one of them sniffed. "And you know what? *Rachel's just like her.*"

Lies. Lies. But how did you fight them when you were fifteen, your mother was dead, your father was the town drunk, your older sister was pregnant and even she didn't know who the father was?

That's what Rachel was thinking about when the restored pink '56 Chevy convertible stopped and Bobby leaned over the imitation leather bench seat to flash his famous dimples. "Hi," he said. "I've been watchin' you and you're gettin' kinda cute. Could you use a lift?"

Rachel didn't hesitate, even though she knew seventeen-year-old Bobby was a hell-raiser much admired locally as "all boy." It didn't hurt that his family was the crème de la crème of Showdown society, either, or that he tossed a mean football in football-mad Texas.

He was not a friend of Rachel's. In fact, she couldn't remember him ever so much as saying hello to her. But on that particular day he was exactly what she needed.

Bobby could sell refrigerators to Eskimos. When he turned on the charm and threw open the car door, Rachel jumped right in....

"Rachel, are you all right?"

She stared blankly at Steve, only belatedly realizing she still stood in the middle of the dance floor although the music had stopped. "I'm sorry," she mumbled, almost cringing before the curious glances. "I just remembered something. Will you excuse me?"

Steve nodded, the very soul of understanding. Rachel picked her way through the crowd to the wide stairs at the back of the room. Seeing Bobby's mother so unexpectedly had unnerved her; that was the only reason she'd succumbed to the bittersweet memories of her secret love.

One foot on the steps, she looked around to find Trey watching her from across the room, his expression...almost compassionate. An electrical force seemed to leap between them, fueled by some secret knowledge on his part. Once again she sensed that he was reading her mind.

Sissy Williams stood beside him, and Rachel felt a pang seeing them together. A perfect pair, she thought disconsolately. Sissy was a divorcée in her early thirties, about Trey's own age. Tall and thin and attractive, she lived with her twin brother Bud, who ran his own spread and worked part-time for the Rocking T.

Sissy was Rachel's opposite—a "good old gal" who went her own way, taking what she wanted, public opinion be damned.

How Rachel envied her!

SISSY WILLIAMS had put Bud up to asking Dixie to dance; Trey knew a setup when he saw one. To his surprise, and perhaps Bud's as well, Dixie accepted. Now Trey stood at the bar with Sissy, watching Rachel disappear up the stairs.

Goddamn, she intrigued the hell out of him. He kept getting little glimpses of what might lurk beneath her surface, and with every tiny taste, the desire for more grew stronger.

Sissy was not pleased. "Could you pay a little attention to me?" she demanded. "I'm the one got rid of Miz Baker so we could get to know each other."

Rachel reached the top of the stairs and passed out of sight. Trey turned back to Sissy. "You don't like Dixie, I take it."

"Dixie, he calls her." Sissy rolled her eyes. "Like has nothin' to do with it." She made a face. "She's nice enough when she wants to be, but when she's riled, look out."

"She seemed to make Rachel nervous." No "seemed" about it; he'd been watching closely; Rachel had taken one look at the woman and unraveled.

"I don't blame Rachel a lick for bein' leery of that woman. Shows she's got good sense. Everyone in town's scared to death of her, so Rachel Cox is hardly alone."

Trey realized with a start that he had never heard Rachel's last name before. "Cox? Did she take back her maiden name?"

"Take it back from where?"

"She's got a kid. Is she widowed, divorced, one of these modern types who never changed her name, what?"

Sissy laughed. "She's never been married. She's always been Rachel Cox."

Rachel the stuffy librarian had had a child out of wedlock? Sissy ought to know, and if it were true...ah, that would certainly explain a lot. "Then who?"

"Then who's the father of her boy?" Sissy looked around with exaggerated care, as if to make sure no one was eavesdropping. She leaned forward, "accidentally" brushing her breasts against his arm. Licking her lips, she gave him a provocative glance. "Nobody knows who the daddy is. Rachel was just a kid herself when . . . Look, I shouldn't be tellin' you all this. Texans are supposed to stick together in dealin's with . . . well . . ."

Trey rolled his eyes. "Yeah, I know. The dreaded damn Yankee ."

Sissy looked distinctly ill at ease. "You promise you won't tell anybody I blabbed?"

"I promise. So say it already."

"Cross your heart and hope to die?"

He groaned. "Sissy. . ."

"Okay, okay, but a girl can't be too careful." She gave him a sideways glance that clearly told him that dictum did not apply to him. "See, Rachel and I went to school together. I was a *tiny* bit older, so we weren't best friends or anything. Well, now I think about it, I'm not sure Rachel had any best friends."

"Why was that?" Would the woman never get to the point?

"I don't know." She shrugged. "Maybe because her daddy was the town drunk, or her sister was the town—" she gave him a quick, assessing glance "—floozy."

Trey let out a low whistle. "You're kidding. Are we talking about the same uptight, upright lady librarian?"

"Ha! You know what they say—fifty percent of an iceberg is underwater." She blinked as if realizing she'd screwed up that analogy, then went blithely on. "When she was fifteen or sixteen, she earned quite a reputation for herself. Then when she turned up pregnant . . . well, I'll give her credit for guts. She kept the baby, and let me tell you that couldn't have been easy—not in this town."

"That'd be Jason." Trey could hardly believe what he was hearing. Rachel was turning out to be even more complex than he'd imagined. And more interesting.

Sissy nodded. "Nice kid. Smart as a whip, I hear."

"So who's the father?"

"Beats me." She frowned. "Now that I think of it, I don't know when she found the time to get into trouble. She was workin' part-time at the Dairy Domicile and had pretty good grades. I'd heard she was hopin' to go to college and then boom! She turns up pregnant."

"But she still managed to get to college," Trey pointed out, his voice soft. He was liking Rachel more because she, too, had faced trials and tribulations without breaking. Maybe she had good reason to be cautious now.

"I heard a rumor that Thom T. Taggart sent her. That'd be just like him. He's always doin' stuff for folks."

"Or to 'em. He took me back into Diablo Canyon the other day, looking for a loose horse, and I came close to breaking my fool neck."

Sissy laughed. "Close only counts in horseshoes." She looked him up and down with the kind of bold consideration he'd relish from Rachel. "I like you," she announced unnecessarily. "After you take Dixie home we could..."

She didn't have to say any more; he knew what they "could." For a moment he considered, or tried to tell himself he was considering.

He wasn't, but saw no reason to hurt Sissy's feelings. He didn't know her very well—Thom T. had introduced them at the bank a day or two ago—but he liked her. He just didn't want to sleep with her...right now.

One more question. "Sissy, when Rachel was in school, did she have a nickname? Most everybody else around here seems to."

Sissy thought for a moment. "Well, it seems to me some of the kids called her... Lisa? Nah, that's not it, but it was an 'L' word. What is her middle name, anyway? I should remember..."

"Elizabeth?" Trey suggested casually.

"That's it. A few of the kids called her Lizzie."

RACHEL HADN'T RETURNED. Although not overtly watching for her, Trey nonetheless was aware of her continuing absence. He glanced over to Dixie, chatting at a table with a couple of women near her own age. Ruby something, who'd been introduced as a quilter and Jenny Merton, a nurse. Sissy was dancing with Steve; Trey wouldn't be missed, he thought as he slipped away from the bar.

Rachel had turned right at the top of the stairs, so he did, too. Rooms opened off either side of a long hallway and it dawned on him that once upon a time this had been a cathouse.

Lace curtains billowed inward from open French doors at the end of the hall and Trey stepped through, onto a balcony running around the side and front of the Yellow Rose.

Directly before him, stairs led down to an alley just off Main Street. Several trash cans were clustered there, along with numerous cardboard boxes awaiting disposal.

To his right, on the longer of the two sections of balcony, he saw several couples necking. To his left, Rachel leaned over the railing on stiff arms, her face lifted toward the full moon.

How had he ever thought her plain? Her face glowed in the moonlight, all graceful symmetry. The ugly brown dress became a darkly magical garment, hinting at the bounty it concealed. For a long moment he simply stared at her. He was getting in way over his head here, but it wasn't in his nature to back away.

He knew he hadn't made a sound, yet she straightened slowly and turned. Leaning back against the railing, she stared at him, the shadows concealing her expression.

"You," she said. She didn't sound surprised.

"Me." Ignoring the tension tightening his body, he walked to stand beside her, next to the stairway. Looking out over Main Street, he added inanely, "Nice party."

"Yes." She hesitated. "How do you happen to know Mrs. Baker?"

"Met her at the restaurant right after I got to town."

"I'm surprised she'd take up with a . . ." Her mouth curved into a smile quickly gone. ". . . stranger."

He slanted her a sardonic glance. "Thanks for not saying the obvious. I think I remind her of her son."

Rachel caught her breath. "Bobby's dead."

"Yeah, I know. Was he a friend of yours?"

Her shrug was barely perceptible. "You could say that."

"But you don't like his mother." It wasn't a question.

"I . . . Let's just say the Bakers and the Coxes have never run in the same social circles." She straightened. "I should be getting back. If you'll excuse me . . ."

He stopped her with a hand on her forearm. "Don't go."

She looked down at his hand but didn't pull away. "I beg your pardon?"

"Okay, *please*. I'd . . . like to hear more about the legend."

She regarded him with suspicion. "I didn't think you believed any of that."

She sounded slightly breathless. Good. And she was trembling beneath his light hold, a hold she could easily break. "I don't," he admitted. "I mean, I didn't but now I'm not sure. Coming here tonight, where *they* were . . . There's something spooky about it. When I walked in I felt . . ."

He slid his hand up her arm, inside the short sleeves of her dress. She shivered, staring at him with eyes that were wide but not yet wary.

"It's almost as if Rose and Jack and Boone are still here," she whispered. "I've always felt their presence very strongly in the Yellow Rose."

"Did nice girls go into places like this, back then?" He slipped his hand smoothly down her arm to her elbow, lightly caressing the sensitive skin at the inner bend. "Rose was a nice girl, I take it."

"The nicest." She swallowed hard. "Under normal circumstances she'd never *ever* have gone into a saloon. But the gunfighter Boone beat up her brother— Thom T.'s grandpa—and broke his arm, so she went lookin' for him. When she found him in the Yellow Rose, she gave him what-for and slapped his face."

It took the merest movement to transfer his hand from her elbow to her waist. "If this Boone was half the man you've made him out to be, he grabbed the impulsive Miss Taggart and taught her a hard lesson."

"He . . . kissed her." She licked her lips.

Trey laughed. "Maybe he really was my great-great-grandfather."

She caught her breath. "You don't understand how horribly humiliating that must have been for her. She had her reputation to think of, her family's standing in the community. According to the social mores of the time, a lady shouldn't even *speak* to a man of his ilk."

"And people call those the good old days," he murmured. With his other hand, he reached out to brush one finger across her cheek. "Now a woman can...*talk*...to anybody she damned well pleases and 'lady' is the dirty word, at least in some circles."

Rachel uttered a small, strangled sound. "You just don't understand how it is in a small town, even now. Once you get a bad reputation..." She bit her lip. "Rose and the sheriff probably left town because her character had been impugned, through no fault of her own. I can understand that, even if you can't."

"It could have been worse." He cupped her face with both hands and stared into her wide eyes.

She covered his hands with her own. "How?"

"Boone Smith could have been a damn Yankee."

"For all I know...he was."

She swayed forward, her eyelids drifting down. He accepted the unconscious invitation and kissed her. He'd thought of doing it for such a long time that he half expected the reality to be anticlimactic.

It wasn't. Her lips, smooth and creamy, parted over a sigh. Desire shot through him and he pulled her against his chest, rushing the pace. His tongue penetrated her mouth and he leaned into her, arching her back against the rail.

The sweetness of her mouth inflamed him. The promise he felt in that fine body pressing so eagerly against his sent fresh tremors of excitement bolting through him. She stirred in his arms, trying to get closer, her breasts and hips rubbing against him. Yeah, oh, yeah, that was it—

"What the hell you think you're doin'?" a hoarse voice demanded; simultaneously, a heavy blow landed between Trey's shoulder blades.

He staggered, trying not to crush Rachel against the rail. He recognized Laddy's voice instantly and turned his head. Drinking again. The boy held a long-necked beer bottle in one hand. This time he'd brought a friend who hovered in the background. The lovers on the other section of the balcony were beginning to take notice.

Trey had no interest in tangling with a couple of drunken kids, although he was sorely tempted, especially considering what they'd just interrupted. If Rachel hadn't been a witness . . . but she was, and a quick glance told him she was mortified.

Laddy brandished the bottle. "I said keep your hands off my sister!"

"No, you said 'What the hell you think you're doin' here?'" *I could wipe up the ground with him*, Trey thought, wanting very much to do that very thing. But if he did, he might as well write off further progress with Rachel, just when things were starting to get interesting.

"Don't change the subject!" Laddy gave Trey a shove. "You got no right to paw my sister."

Rachel groaned. "Laddy Cox, go away and mind your own business. I can take care of myself." She glanced unhappily at their audience.

"You were doin' a piss-poor job of it, judgin' by what I just saw." Laddy hefted his beer bottle, his eyes narrowing dangerously. "Guess it's up to me to teach this damn Yankee a lesson."

He hauled back the bottle and brought it down with all his might, aiming squarely for Trey's head.

6

THE BOTTLE in Laddy's hand descended in an arc, the boy's stupidity offering Trey an opportunity too good to pass up. At the very last instant, he tilted his head just enough to let the bottle glance harmlessly off the side of his face and onto his shoulder, where it struck with a solid thwack!

Groaning loudly, he stumbled back dramatically to teeter on the stair behind him. Playing it for all it was worth, he windmilled his arms as if fighting for balance.

In fact, he'd already decided to do a pratfall down the stairs. With boxes and cans to break his descent at the bottom, it should be a piece of cake.

A bruise or two was a small price to pay to impress a woman and scare the crap out of a damn fool kid, all in one fell swoop.

PARALYZED WITH HORROR, Rachel watched Trey plunge backward off the balcony and careen from side to side and end over end down the flight of stairs. He landed flat on his back in the middle of trash cans and cardboard boxes and lay very still.

Laddy's exclamation pierced the shocked silence. "Shit! I think I killed the son of a—"

"We are in big trouble," Virgil wailed. "We'll rot in jail for this one!"

Rachel shoved the two aside and hurled herself down the stairs. Clinging to the handrails, she almost slid to the bottom, where she dropped to her knees beside Trey's inert form. Grabbing handfuls of his white silk shirt, she stared into his face, praying.

Laddy and the other witnesses clustered around. "My God, did you see that?" someone exclaimed in an awed tone. "He must have broken every bone in his body."

Trey let out an agonized groan, the first sound he'd made since going over the edge, but didn't open his eyes.

Rachel tightened her grip on his shirt. "I think he's coming around!" she cried with more hope than certainty. "Trey, speak to me—please speak to me!"

He rolled his head to one side and groaned again. His eyelashes flickered. "Wh-what happened?"

She looked into the starlit sky and uttered a heartfelt, "Thank you, God." Cupping Trey's face between her hands, she pleaded, "Tell me where it hurts. Did you break anything?"

"I . . . I'm okay." He sounded weak and disoriented but not in terrible pain. "What happened?"

"You slipped and fell, man!" Virgil stumbled over the lie, and a disapproving murmur rose from the witnesses.

"The hell you did!" Laddy glared at his victim. He was trying to act macho but his trembling voice gave him away. "I hit you!"

"And you damned well better be sorry!" Rachel was so angry the swear word slipped out. "You better get down on your knees and thank God you didn't kill him. And while you're at it, you owe Trey an abject apology."

"I don't owe him jack—"

Trey's tortured groan cut off the argument; he tried to rise. Rachel pushed him back down, making soothing little sounds. "Will someone help me get him inside so he can be comfortable while we send for the doctor?" she asked.

Trey caught her forearm with startling strength. "No doctors. Just let me rest a few minutes. I'll ... be all right."

She wanted desperately to believe him but found it difficult, considering the fall he'd taken. "Are you sure?"

"Pretty sure." He wriggled uncomfortably on the smashed cardboard boxes. "If you could just...elevate my head a little...."

That was simple; she sat down and eased his head onto her lap, then glared at her brother. "Bring him a glass of water and then you and your simian friend can get lost. You've done quite enough for one evening."

Trey tugged at her hand and she looked down anxiously. "You want something else? Have you changed your mind about the doctor?"

"Could you ... could you get everyone to go away?" He rolled his eyes to indicate their audience. "They're staring at me."

They certainly were, but when they heard his painful whisper they took the hint and retreated, albeit reluctantly and with many a backward glance. They'd be talking about this for a long time, she knew to her chagrin. But Trey wouldn't care and she couldn't think of herself, not now.

Laddy returned with the glass of water. "I'm out of here," he announced, giving the prostrate man a sullen glance. "He's okay."

"You'd better hope. We'll talk about this later, Laddy Cox." Rachel slid her arm beneath Trey's head and lifted the glass of water to his lips.

With his head resting quite naturally in the crook of her arm, he drank. Then he sighed and closed his eyes, his head lolling against her... against her breast. Had he lost consciousness again? She dared not move, she dared not breathe... she dared not think about the proximity of his mouth to her nipple.

That was the only thing Trey *could* think about. He felt her soft flesh tighten and knew that with the most minute move... His own body clenched in anticipation.

This time his groan was utterly sincere. Jeez, he should have gone home with Sissy. This kind of frustration couldn't be good for a man, even for a cause as worthy as scaring the shit out of a couple of kids who richly deserved it.

With jerky movements that bespoke stress, she lowered his head back onto her lap, which wasn't that bad a deal, either. "Is... is there anything else I can do for you?" she faltered.

Hell, yes! He could think of dozens, but they all worked better naked. He drew in a quivering breath. "Not for me, but... Thom T. needs..."

"What? What does he need?"

He spoke with agonizing slowness. "Thom T. needs... wants you and your kid to come stay with him so you can... find out the truth... about everything." *That's right, nice dark tone.*

"Oh, that's not really a very good—"

"*Please?* You know and I know I'm no Taggart, but Thom T... Well, the longer this drags on, the harder it'll be for him to accept that. Do it for *him*, Rachel."

She caught her breath and he saw her waver. She didn't trust him as far as she could throw him, but she also felt responsible for his present plight. How could she possibly turn him down?

She couldn't. Her shoulders slumped. "All right. I guess it's the least I can do under the circumstances."

"That's a promise?" *Easy, man, don't sound too eager—or too strong.*

"It's a promise." Said reluctantly, but said.

He held up one hand and she automatically took it into her own, twining her fingers through his. "In that case," he whispered, so low she had to lean forward to hear him, "let's seal the deal."

He slid one hand around the back of her head and pulled her flat onto his chest. His hot mouth took hers, his tongue plunging inside before she could react.

Caught completely by surprise, she kissed him back, swept away on a tide of passionate yearning. She couldn't believe she was doing this, yet longed to do more, such as ripping off his clothes to ravish his poor, wounded body.

Poor, wounded body? It didn't act wounded, nor did it feel that way where it pressed against hers. One of his arms clamped across her back like an iron bar, crushing her breasts against his unyielding chest. The other curved around her neck like a vise.

Trey Smith must have the most raging libido in the history of mankind to make a move on her while still half out of his mind with pain—he might even have a concussion, she thought groggily.

She'd certainly never dreamed a kiss so demanding, yet so coaxing, could be over so quickly. Or that a man who'd just fallen down an entire flight of stairs could spring to his feet and smile down at her while she sat dazed and muddled on crushed cardboard boxes in an alley.

"It's a miracle," he declared, an undercurrent of laughter in his voice. "I'm cured!" He grabbed her hands and pulled her to her feet.

She'd been conned. She didn't know how—she'd seen him fall with her own eyes—but he'd definitely taken an unfair advantage.

Nevertheless, she'd given her word and would keep it.

RACHEL AND JASON moved to the Rocking T the next day.

The boy was delighted, which surprised Rachel. He'd never been an outdoors-type kid; his surroundings had never seemed important to him one way or the other. Stowing his belongings in his temporary bedroom, he took off to explore, without the omnipresent book.

Rachel watched him go before following Thom T. into his library-study to receive the mass of material collected by the late P.I.

The old man looked enormously relieved. "Cain't tell you how much I appreciate this, Rachel gal," he said.

"It's nothing," she lied. "I owe you so much, I'll never be able to repay it."

"Hogwash." He waved her gratitude aside. "I wouldn't trust just anyone to do this. Not that I don't know what you'll find."

"Well, if you know, why—?"

"To satisfy *him*."

She didn't have to ask who. "But you're almost certain to be disappointed," she argued. "Trey himself says there's no way he could be related to you."

Thom T. snorted. "How in Hades would he know? He never had nobody to call his own and he's afraid to admit he wants to." The lined face softened. "But he does."

"How can you be so sure of that, Thom T.? Trey strikes me as a pretty self-contained individual."

"Because *everybody* wants somebody to call his own. Otherwise, what's the use a'goin' on?" His eyes took on a crafty gleam. "And that includes you, missy. You ain't near as satisfied as you let on."

She raised her chin. "I don't know what you're talking about."

But she did, and he was right; she was anything but satisfied. For years—ever since Bobby—she'd kept the passionate side of her nature under lock and key. Now Trey Smith had come along with his bold good looks and brash manner to threaten everything she'd worked so hard to achieve.

Satisfied? Not anymore.

TREY GAVE THE BUCKSKIN a pat on the rump and watched the horse bound away. Old Buck was feeling good these days. Might be about time to put him back to work.

Jason, hanging on the top rail of the corral, jumped down to stand beside Trey. "You act like a tenderfoot," the boy observed, "but you're not. What'd you say you did in California?"

Trey laughed and looked at the boy with affection, realized what he was doing and forced a frown. "I didn't say."

The boy's grin grew wider. "You don't have to," he said confidently. "Can I ride your horse?"

"No, and he's not my horse. He's Thom T.'s horse."

"I think he's your horse. And I think he's the horse you were ridin' when you got hurt." The boy gave the man a mischievous glance.

"This I gotta hear." Trey ambled over to the corral and leaped halfway up, then climbed the rest of the way to perch on the top rail.

The boy joined him. "It's like this. Sometimes I . . . hear things."

"Eavesdrop, you mean."

"Yeah, maybe." Jason's face beamed with angelic innocence. "I've picked up a lot about you."

"Such as?" Trey's curiosity grew.

"That you come from California, that you got hurt fallin' off a horse. . . ."

That was what he'd told Liz that night in the cantina and she must have repeated it. No one else knew that besides Thom T.

"That you work for a movie company, but not as an actor, that you can swing through the trees like Tarzan."

"How the hell do you know that?" Trey demanded. "You weren't there to see old Fluffy make a fool out of me."

"Sure I was. I was watching outa my bedroom window. You just didn't see me, is all."

"Sneaky little—" Trey started to ruffle the boy's dark hair, but stopped.

Jason slanted a look of admiration at his companion. "I heard about what happened at the Yellow Rose. Everybody in town's talkin' about it. I'm surprised nobody else's figured it out. I guess most of 'em just see a damn Yankee and don't look any further."

"Figured out what, hotshot?"

"That you're a Hollywood stuntman," the boy said ingenuously. "I figure you got hurt doin' a gag for a picture and that's why...."

Trey was so surprised he nearly fell off the corral rail. "What the hell do you know about gags?" he demanded.

The boy shrugged. "Library research. When I ask my mother questions, she always says, 'Look it up.' So I—"

"Jeez, you won't mention this to your mother!" It'd ruin everything; Rachel wouldn't take kindly to being suckered by that fall at the Yellow Rose last weekend. When bent on seduction, a man didn't... *Seduction?* How could he sit here next to the child of his object of desire and think about *seduction?* He jumped down and glared at the boy through slitted eyes.

Jason's face trembled. "I didn't say a word about this to my mother," he protested hurriedly. "I researched it myself. I know my way around a library pretty damn good."

"Don't swear."

The narrow jaw jutted out. "You swear."

"I'm a grown-up. You're just a kid—and a smart-assed kid at that."

"What're you so mad about? I haven't done anything." Jason blinked hard; he looked to be on the verge of tears.

Trey refused to let himself soften. If Rachel realized he was playing games with her and her brother . . . No, he couldn't let that happen. He wanted to level with her but would have to pick his time.

In the meanwhile, he needed the boy's promise not to say anything to anyone, not even to his mother, even if that meant lying to her.

But he couldn't. Goddamn it, he couldn't ask a boy to lie to his mother. So he just said, "I don't like people poking their noses into my business, and that includes kids."

He turned and walked away, feeling like a real shit.

TREY'S BAD MOOD was still firmly in place at dinnertime. A telephone call, coming between the main course and dessert, took Rachel away from the table and did nothing to improve the unhappy atmosphere.

After a few minutes, Thom T.'s impatience got the better of him and he stamped away, muttering under his breath. Trey and Jason sat there, waiting, but not patiently. The boy kept his attention on his plate. Trey, who knew why, fumed.

Suddenly the boy looked up. "I didn't say anything to my mom," he blurted. "I can keep a secret."

"So can she, apparently."

"Huh?"

"Who's your father, Jason? What happened to him?" Trey hadn't been aware how much those two questions had been preying on his mind.

Jason glanced anxiously toward the door through which Rachel had exited. "I'm not supposed to talk about that."

"Then you do know who he was?"

"Yes . . . no. I mean, Mom said she'd explain all that when I'm older." He jumped to his feet. "Please excuse me."

"Jason, wait! I'm sorry."

Too late; the boy was gone. Trey rose, wondering if he'd ever learn to keep his big mouth shut. Apparently not, he decided, beginning to stack the dishes. Elva What's-her-name, Thom T.'s housekeeper, had cooked and gone home, leaving cleanup to the diners, as was the custom.

Trey, who'd grown up self-reliant, had no problem with that. He could scrape a plate or wash a dish with the best of them.

Rachel apparently found that rather shocking, judging by her expression when she walked in a few minutes later and saw what he was doing. She carried a tray bearing four dessert dishes filled with tapioca pudding.

"I'm sorry that took so long." She placed the dishes on the table. "Laddy . . ."

Trey put down his stack of dirty dishes and reached for dessert. "Laddy what?" he prompted her, sitting down.

She shrugged uncertainly. "Nothing." After a moment, she, too, sat down and picked up a spoon.

"So what kind of trouble's your brother in now?"

A flush swept over her cheekbones, tinting her olive complexion with rose. She had beautiful skin, smooth and clear and soft looking. Damn it, he shouldn't be rhapsodizing about skin. If he chose to think about her at all, he should be speculating in far more graphic terms. He shifted uncomfortably, suddenly conscious that he'd let his thoughts stray a mite too far south.

"Laddy's not in trouble," she said defensively. "His car's on the blink and he just wanted to borrow mine."

"Which you wisely refused."

"Yes." She bit her lip. "Look, I know you detest my brother, and after what he did, I don't blame you."

"I don't detest him."

"Hate him, then."

"Wrong again."

Her hazel eyes flashed green fire. "Damnation! Then you tell me!"

Trey savored her outburst even more than his tapioca. "I don't care about him one way or another. I will admit that generally speaking, I don't like drunks."

She caught her breath. "He's not a drunk. But even if he were, that's a terribly cruel thing to say. You just don't know how hard it's been for him."

She stopped, eyes widening. He could see how afraid she was that she might say too much.

"I do know," he said. "Your father was the town drunk. So what? At least you and your brother *had* a father. Not everybody's so lucky."

As soon as Trey heard his words, he knew he'd made a mistake. He'd meant to indicate that her father's reputation cast no shadow upon her, her brother or her son, unless they let it. He'd also been obliquely referring to himself.

But when she glanced at Jason's empty chair, he sensed that he'd called attention to the lack of a father in her son's life. "I didn't mean that like it sounded," he hastily amended—too late, for she was rising to her feet.

She spoke in a carefully controlled voice. "You know nothing about me or my family, so I'd really appreciate it if you'd keep your opinions to yourself."

"I couldn't agree with you more." *Butt out, Smith.* "Only thing is, you don't know what trouble your brother's headed for if something doesn't turn him around. And that's fact, not opinion. You'll be lucky if he doesn't kill himself, or someone else."

"That's enough! You have no right—"

"Yeah, well, the truth often hurts."

Giving him a last, harried glance, she scooped up the dishes he'd stacked and marched into the kitchen. Trey grabbed a couple of glasses and followed.

She set the dishes upon the counter and turned so suddenly that he bumped into her. "Why?" she demanded, her tone plaintive now. "Why do you say such horrible things? What makes you such an expert on my brother?"

"Experience. I've known too many like him." Trey placed the water glasses in the sink and flexed his hands; this wasn't the time to make a move on her, yet he found himself reaching for her just the same. He draped his hands on the upper curves of her shoulders, thumbs stroking her collarbone.

She held her breath and stared at him. Her skin was warm and supple and her pulse pounded beneath his light touch, betraying her excitement. No matter how calm she might look, inside she was feeling the heat just as he was.

Old hurts and new longings clashed. "Alcohol's your brother's drug of choice, but it could just as easily be coke or crack or crystal meth or anything else he could shoot up or drop down."

Wrapped up in his own physical reactions, Trey had spoken without thinking. He dropped his hands to his side, a little shocked at what he was telling her. "Look," he said roughly, "I didn't intend to get into this, but you asked. I don't care what he does or doesn't do. As you so aptly pointed out, it's none of my business."

"But you do care. I just don't understand why."

Bitter experience motivated his denial. "The hell I do. My only interest in the entire Cox family is getting you into bed with me and you damned well know it."

Her mouth dropped open and her eyes grew wide with shock. He watched with satisfaction but little understanding. He'd changed the subject and regained the upper hand, and that was enough for the moment.

Rachel threw back her shoulders and glared at him. "I'm going to forget you said that," she announced in a strangled voice. "I'll thank you never to suggest such a thing again."

"Grow up," he snapped. "We're consenting adults." He almost added, *Liz.*

"I don't consent, and I never will." She was trembling. "What do you think I am? I'd never risk my reputation ag—"

He knew she had caught herself just in time.

"—for some fast-talking Yankee con artist."

"Wait a minute, wait a minute." He pressed his palms to his temples. "I think I'm getting a flash of déjà vu here. What century are we in? Is your name Rose Taggart? Are you waiting for me to beat up your brother before I carry you away or—?"

She silenced him by planting one heel solidly on the toes exposed by his right sandal. He interpreted that as an unqualified *No!*

But then, he wasn't a man to take no for an answer, he thought, hopping around on one foot while massaging the bruised toes of the other. How would Boone the Mysterious Gunfighter have handled this?

IT WAS ALMOST TEN O'CLOCK that night when the sheriff's car drove past Trey's little house, taking the shortcut to the ranch headquarters. Without hesitation, he leaped off the porch where he'd been contemplating the beauty of the night sky and took off after the red taillights that were dropping over the hill.

He ran joyfully, oxygen streaming through his lungs. He should have tried exercise sooner, he realized as his muscles warmed and stretched and his stride lengthened. All his excess energy—sexual energy—welcomed the release that action brought.

By leaving the dirt road and cutting across a field, he arrived at the big house only a minute or two behind the cop. Rachel must have heard the car, for she stood on the steps, waiting.

"What is it, Pete?" Trey heard her say as he jogged up.

The wiry police officer gave him a quick glance before answering. "It's Laddy."

Rachel's hand flew to her throat. "Oh, God, tell me he's not—?"

"Nah, he's not hurt," the officer reassured her, although he sounded disgusted.

"Then what?"

Pete shuffled his feet. "I'm sorry to tell you this, Rachel, but we got your brother in jail."

"Jail! But why? What for?"

"Grand theft auto. He took Dub Partridge's big ol' pickup truck and—"

"Oh, my God! You scared me, Pete." Rachel slumped with relief. "There's been some mistake. Dub's twin boys are friends of Laddy's. Dub would never..."

Pete shook his head. "Sorry, that don't wash. Dub is good and mad—says Laddy asked to borrow the truck and when he turned him down, the boy waited till Dub's back was turned and hot-wired the damned thing. If Laddy thinks this is some kind of lark, I'm afraid he's got another think comin'."

"If Dub drops charges, will that be enough to straighten this whole thing out?"

Pete hesitated and Trey held his breath. Damn, she was making a helluva mistake. Let the boy learn, if learning was in him.

Pete exhaled slowly. "I guess so, but Rachel, I gotta tell you I don't think that's such a good idea...."

He was talking to thin air; Rachel had turned to run back inside. Pete looked at Trey and shrugged. "He ain't a bad kid," he said plaintively, "but that woman keeps bailin' him outa one scrape after another. Sooner or later, he's gonna have to pay the piper."

"Ain't it the truth." Trey stuck out his hand. "Name's Trey Smith."

Pete shook hands. "Yeah, I know. Been meanin' to say howdy. Heard some talk around town about you." A slight pause, then he added, "Any of it true?"

Trey laughed. "Probably. The bad part, anyhow."

The officer nodded. "That's what I thought till Miz Baker started singin' your praises. Now I ain't so sure."

"Up to you." Trey shrugged. "About Laddy Cox..."

The screen door flew open and Rachel hurried out. "I spoke to Dub and he's agreed to let Laddy off this time," she announced.

"This time?" The officer's disgust was plain. "Rachel, I swear, I don't know what I'm gonna do with you if you don't quit babying that boy!" He slapped his hands on the ammo belt around his waist. "I'm wastin' my breath."

He turned and stalked back to his patrol car. Trey watched, wondering how anyone was going to get through to Rachel.

She beat him to the punch. "Don't say it—just don't say it. I'm not even vaguely interested in your opinion."

She stood two steps above him, wearing a nightgown and robe of some thin, summery material. By the silvery moonlight, he could see that her hair was plaited loosely in a single braid that hung down her back. He saw her waver beneath his gaze, crossing her arms over her breast as if to protect herself.

"If you're not interested in anything I have to say, maybe you'll be interested in what I plan to do."

He let the words roll out, full and soft with promise, without any of the half-joking quality that had so often marked his dealings with her. She stood as still and straight as a statue, not softening even when he drew her to the edge of the step. He reached beneath her nightgown with both hands, stroking up the fullness of her bare calves, at the same time pressing the side of his face to her abdomen beneath her folded arms.

Rachel's head fell back and she stared unseeingly at the sky. This couldn't be happening. He was touching her, exactly the way she longed to be touched. She needed his hands on her. *Yes!* Stroking over trembling thighs bare beneath her gown . . .

His dark head pressed against her midriff just below her breasts. She wanted so much to remove the barrier of her crossed arms but couldn't find the courage.

With a provocative slowness he lowered her to the next step, the top of his head nudging aside her arms. She couldn't breathe, waiting to see what he would do next, praying it would be what she wanted but was too cowardly to request.

His seeking mouth fumbled against her, then closed over one straining nipple. Her breasts had ached for this, longed for this. She had never been touched quite this way. She'd never known a man's lovemaking, only a boy's. That glimpse, so powerful at the time, had not prepared her for the intensity of this heedless pleasure, spiraling from her throbbing breasts to the deepest recesses of her body, to the empty, aching, needy place inside.

Without any idea how it happened, she found herself straddling his bare thigh and dimly became aware that he'd placed his foot on the bottom step. Instinctively she held on to his shoulders and arched her back, spreading her thighs and lifting her breasts toward his clever, seeking tongue.

She wanted to do things with him she couldn't even name. Mindless with wanting, she felt the shattering of her vaunted self-control and the blossoming of passion she'd ruthlessly suppressed for a very long time.

He caught one nipple between his teeth and tugged, setting off another series of deep, quivering contractions that made her groan. His hands roamed over her, kneading and molding her buttocks, touching her with intimate understanding.

He lifted his mouth from her breast and she moaned a protest. "Let's go back to my place," he said in a strangled voice. "What I want from you—what I want to give you is going to take a long...slow...loving...time."

"I...can't." The denial sprang automatically from the discipline of years. "This isn't right...."

"Sure it is."

His nimble fingers inserted themselves between his flesh and hers. The white heat of desire shuddered through her and she shifted ever so slightly to give him better access. He molded his palm to her contours while little, wordless gasps and tremors shook her.

And he knew, he understood without words what she was feeling. Stroking, teasing, he pleased her until she thought she'd die of it. She burned. He bore her weight while her hips rocked against his muscular thigh and possessive fingers. Spasms shook her, grew harder and faster, and he matched her pace....

She exploded into a fierce orgasm, then clung weakly to the powerful shoulders of the man who had pulled this response from the very depths of her soul.

And as the vibrations receded, she wondered how she would find the strength to resist him now.

7

LADDY PACED around Thom T.'s library, digging his boot heels into the Oriental carpet. "Don't hold your breath waiting for me to thank you, Lizzie. Dub wasn't really gonna press charges."

Rachel glared at her brother across the stacks of paper littering her worktable. After her cataclysmic encounter with Trey last night, Laddy's complaints struck her as juvenile and ill-timed. "Don't be flippant," she snapped. "And don't call me Lizzie."

Laddy made a face; he wasn't taking any of this seriously. For a second she flashed on Trey's warning that her brother was headed for trouble, but almost instantly that memory melted into other, more erotic images.

What had gotten into her last night? Trey had touched her and she'd ignited, splintering the self-control she'd worked so hard to attain. Like Caesar's wife, she must be above suspicion—even her own.

Yet the passionate nature that had brought her to grief once before still simmered beneath the surface. It frightened her to recognize the fact. She'd spent years suppressing the part of herself awakened by Bobby Baker; now Trey Smith had come along and... She shook her head, unwilling to confront her feelings.

Laddy was her immediate problem, not Trey. "Dub had every intention of pressing charges," she said. "He was madder than a wet hen. I had to do some fast talking to calm him down."

Laddy's lip curled. "I'll bet the California flash was right there, tellin' you to let me rot in jail."

She gave him a quick glance. "Deputy Snow said the same thing."

Laddy took another swig from his can of soda. "That damn Yankee's been against me from the git-go," he said, clearly choosing to ignore her mention of the deputy. "I don't know who the hell he thinks he is."

"What difference does it make? You're the one who took Dub's truck." She hesitated. "You were drinking, weren't you."

"I wasn't drunk, if that's what you think." His eyes flashed. "Why can't you leave me alone, Lizzie? I'm not a baby. I don't need you motherin' me like some wet-behind-the-ears kid."

He paced to the window and peered past the heavy green drapes. "No damn Yankee tenderfoot is gonna come in here bad-mouthin' me and get away with it," he muttered. "I'll get even."

Rachel groaned. "Revenge isn't the answer."

"The hell it isn't." He thrust his hands into the pockets of his Levi's, looking suddenly very young and very vulnerable. "I don't know why everybody's always on my case, anyway. I don't drink any more than my friends. Take Virgil—he drinks more'n I do."

"But alcohol affects him differently." Laddy had never before come this close to discussing his consumption of alcohol with her. Was this progress? She felt a little leap of hope and hurried on. "And Virge's father didn't die an alcoholic. Oh, Laddy, it really scares me to see you comin' home the way Daddy used to."

"I don't! Pa was a mean drunk and I'm nothin' like that."

"You're gettin' to be. If you'd just cut down for your own sake—"

"Don't tell me what to do!"

"Okay, okay, calm down. If you won't do it for yourself and you won't do it for me, how about cutting back for Jason's sake?"

Laddy glared at her. Dark circles beneath his eyes attested to a bad night. Although Rachel had never endured a hangover, she'd seen her father suffer through enough of them to recognize one a mile away.

"What about Jason?" Laddy snarled. "I'd never do anything to hurt the kid. You know that."

She nodded. "I know you wouldn't hurt him *deliberately*. But you're setting such a bad example, Laddy. He looks up to you—"

"Hah! Jason looked up to me before *he* came to town. You notice how the kid follows him around like a little ol' hound puppy? Well, I'm gonna take care of that."

Laddy stormed out, leaving Rachel to ponder his final declaration. He was determined to discredit Trey in Jason's eyes, those of the city of Showdown and the state of Texas, if at all possible. Although she didn't know what he had in mind, she should warn Trey....

Or should she? Trey himself had told her to mind her own business. Trey and Laddy could take care of themselves.

Unlike me. Again that scene last night on the ranch house steps flashed into her head . . . she swallowed hard. How could she have behaved so shamelessly? She doubted she'd ever be able to look Trey Smith in the face again, let alone carry on a polite conversation with him.

LADDY COX was up to something; he was acting too civilly not to be. Grateful for even that diversion, Trey waited for the kid to make his move.

Anything to take his mind off Rachel. He'd been an idiot the other night, putting her needs ahead of his own. Once again he'd proven where nice guys finished.

He'd also proven that she was as wildly passionate as he'd suspected, if considerably less experienced. Now he wanted her so damned bad his teeth—and other things—ached, while she was barely speaking to him, and then only in the line of duty.

Thom T. had set her a helluva task, sorting through all the crap that detective had gathered. Jeez, she even had copies of Trey's old elementary school report cards and a lace and paper valentine he'd made one of his foster mothers when he was in the second or third grade.

She didn't have a copy of his birth certificate, but he couldn't help her there. He didn't recall ever seeing such a document himself. He could only assume one had been produced when he first entered school, thereby documenting his age and existence for all eternity.

Trey was doing pull-ups on the bar mounted between two trees when Rachel and Tom T. came out of the house, saw him and paused. He gave them a cocky grin and a phony count, "Eighty-seven, eighty-eight," which brought a laugh from Jason, an admiring audience.

Clamping one arm behind his waist, Trey threw in a couple of one-armers before dropping to the ground. Grabbing his T-shirt from a nearby limb, he swiped at his sweaty face and grinned.

Rachel rolled her eyes. "Jason, are you ready to go?"

"Can I come later with Uncle Laddy?"

Trey could see her trying not to look at him. "I suppose that'll be all right." She turned away.

Thom T. clapped his white Stetson upon his head. "Sure you won't change your mind?" he asked Trey. "No big shakes, just a lotta the boys workin' their old ropin' horses. Whole town shows up—women sell eats, kids run around like little heathens. Good clean fun."

Trey grimaced. "Not my favorite kind. I'll pass." He watched Rachel closely. There was something different about her, some new vulnerability, a new softness of expression, try though she might to conceal it.

He had uncovered her secrets and was prepared to exploit them. She was ripe and ready and wouldn't be able to hold him off much longer.

"Up to you." Thom T. started toward the car. "I told Laddy he could truck a coupla horses to town. When he shows up, don't run him off."

"Me?" Trey watched Rachel stretch over the hood of the Cadillac to wipe off the windshield, her tan slacks curving over that compact little backside. His gut clenched and he forgot whatever bantering thing he had meant to say to the old man.

By the time Laddy and Virge came putt-putting up in Laddy's old black Mustang, Trey's mood had gone past restlessness to agitation. He loitered nearby while they hooked a horse trailer to Thom T.'s pickup, amused by their heavy-handed attempts to interest him in the day's enterprise.

Laddy loaded a couple of roping horses and closed the trailer door, giving Trey a shifty-eyed glance. "Sure you don't wanna change your mind and come along? Might be a coupla laughs in it for you."

"You know," Trey drawled, "I think I might. I'll just jump in the back of the pickup and ride along."

"Nah, don't do that." Laddy licked his lips. "That's illegal, seat belt laws and all. You can drive my car."

He must have had his hand on the key chain in his pocket, so quickly did he produce it. He flipped the keys through the air. "My Mustang gets a little bit temperamental once in a while, but nothin' a good driver can't handle."

Trey caught the key chain. "Thanks. Maybe Jason wants to ride with me."

"No!" Laddy exchanged a quick glance with Virgil. "I mean, there's enough room for him in the pickup. I ain't seen much of the kid lately—you understand."

Yeah, Trey understood.

"You know the way to the rodeo grounds?" Laddy inquired solicitously.

"South side of town, right?"

"There's a shortcut that'll bring you in the back way." Laddy licked his lips. "Turn right at the Turners' mailbox and you'll wind around on a little ol' road down a little ol' hill that comes out at the back of the arena." Another shifty exchange of glances with Virge and he added, "That's the way we're goin'. See you there."

The "little old road" Laddy had described was called Dead Man's Curve and with good reason. Trey fingered the keys, hoping he knew what he was doing; he was pretty sure he knew what Laddy was doing. Or trying to do, anyway.

After looking beneath the hood of Laddy's Mustang junker, all doubts disappeared. Whistling beneath his breath, Trey made his preparations. What he was planning needed to be spectacular and it needed to happen in full view of as many townsmen as possible.

Dead Man's Curve. Perfect.

"HERE HE COMES! Damn, he made it all the way to the top!" Laddy pointed toward the hairpin road leading up the steep grade from the back entrance of the rodeo grounds. "How the hell'd that damn Yankee nurse that piece a junk all the way from the Rocking T?"

Sure enough, the little Mustang chugged along, already beginning the long, steep descent.

Virgil elbowed Rachel in the ribs. "Your brother's a real card," he chortled. "That Yankee won't know what hit him."

Rachel twisted around on her seat in the bleachers and stared toward the car in the distance. Trey, driving Laddy's car? It made no sense.

Was it her imagination, or did the car seem to be picking up speed? Had Laddy warned Trey about the Mustang's bad brakes and other mechanical problems? Surely Laddy hadn't intended anything—anything potentially *fatal*?

She glanced at her brother and it seemed to her his face had turned pale. She leaned forward and clutched his hand; it was icy cold.

A murmur went through the sparse crowd as more and more people became aware of the rapidly approaching vehicle. "Who's the maniac?" somebody wondered, and the answer reverberated through the stands: "Damn Yankee!"

"He's coming too fast, Laddy!" Rachel squeezed his hand in her agitation. "He'll flip when he hits the gravel at the bottom."

"Hah-hah-hah!" Virgil pounded one big fist on Laddy's back. "You said you'd fix his little red wagon, and it sure looks like you done it this time!"

Shayne and Dwayne Partridge, Dub's twin boys, hauled around, surprise on their broad faces. "You done that?" Shayne demanded, jerking a thumb toward the hill. "Man, you got guts!"

Maybe he'd thought he had at the time, but now Laddy just looked sick. Shaking off his sister, he jumped to the ground and trotted toward the foot of the hill, where Trey would eventually arrive, in one piece or in many.

Where was Jason? Rachel looked around and finally spotted him behind the chutes with a group of other boys. Satisfied that he wouldn't be a witness to the possible disaster, she hurried after her brother.

Trey could be killed. Her heart skipped a beat and then began a frantic pounding. What had begun as Laddy's childish prank was about to turn deadly. If anything happened to Trey, she would never forgive her brother—or herself.

She began to run.

The car hurtled down the twisting road. He'd never be able to control it when he hit the gravel at the bottom, assuming he didn't overshoot the last curve and tumble end over end down a twenty- or thirty-foot drop-off.

It wasn't called Dead Man's Curve for nothing. People had died on that treacherous hill.

He took the final curve on two wheels, so close to the edge that the tires flung a spray of gravel over the precipice. The car careened down the final stretch. Maybe he could still make it....

It was too much to hope for. Traveling at top speed, the car hit the gravel and went into a spin. Then something happened, Rachel didn't know what. Perhaps it struck a rock or the brakes locked, but for whatever reason, the vehicle flipped and began to roll and roll and roll....

A collective gasp rose from the onlookers, who were becoming horribly aware that nobody could live through such a spectacular misadventure. With a final, shuddering bang, the Mustang came to rest right side up, landing so hard that dust exploded into a curtain around it.

The crowd seemed rooted to the spot by the awfulness of what it had witnessed. Before anyone could even move, the dust cloud shifted and Trey Smith emerged, coughing and brushing in vain at the brown film settling on his hot-orange T-shirt and artfully ragged jeans.

He glanced at Laddy, who was standing nearest to the now-totaled car, and tossed the keys through the air. "Sorry about that," he said cheerfully. "Hope you've got insurance."

"By the way, those brakes are shot."

LADDY SURE WAS GOING to wonder what the hell the ropes and pillows were doing under the front seat of his car—assuming he ever looked, Trey thought as he walked toward Rachel. She looked on the verge of collapse.

In all likelihood, the kid'd have the car towed and sold for junk, which was what it mostly had been before and *sure* was now.

Trey stopped in front of Rachel, who continued to stare at him with parted lips and glazed eyes. "I sure could use something cold to drink," he announced. "Hot day."

She took a sharp breath. "How did you do that?"

He glanced toward the car, now surrounded by an awed circle of men and boys. "Do what?"

"You know 'do what.' You just walked away from a crash that would have killed a—" she bit her lower lip, then finished defensively "—a normal human being!"

"Just lucky," he said modestly, enjoying her bewilderment. "About that drink . . ."

"Lemme buy." It was Laddy, his manner eager and conciliating. "Man, that was close. Lemme buy you a drink, somethin' to eat." He gestured toward a banner drooping above a wooden booth, proclaiming it an enterprise of the Volunteer Fire Department Auxiliary.

Why not? Trey needed to keep his strength up; something told him he hadn't seen the last of Laddy's "pranks."

"HERE, TRY THIS," Laddy urged.

"Is it hot?" Trey peered dubiously at the red stuff in the plastic foam bowl.

"That's good chili, made by these fine ladies here," Laddy protested. "Hey, it's just a little bit spicy, is all. Nothin' a *man* can't handle."

Trey glanced from Laddy to Dixie Baker and her friend, Ruby, working inside the booth. Rachel stood to one side, looking at him a trifle strangely. The expression of the other observers could only be classified as expectant.

As for the contents of his bowl, how hot could it be? Dixie would warn him, right? California had Mexican food, too.

"I believe you, kid," Trey lied. He shoveled a spoonful into his mouth and chewed thoughtfully before swallowing. Going down it felt like a glowing briquette of charcoal, and he suspected his face must be turning a vivid scarlet.

"Good, huh?" Laddy prodded, his expression wicked. He plunged his elbow into Virge's side, eliciting a grunt.

"Damn good." Quickly Trey inhaled the rest of the bowlful, knowing he'd give himself away if he chugalugged his cup of iced tea first. The cold liquid, when it finally came, slid down his burning throat like nectar.

He gulped a mouthful of air. The drink hadn't put out all the fire, but something curious seemed to be happening: his throat was going numb. He heard someone mutter, "Goddamn, he may be a damn Yankee, but he's sure as hell a *red-blooded* damn Yankee!"

Trey grinned cockily. "How about one more for the road?" he requested, holding out his bowl. His throat was so paralyzed he couldn't feel his own vocal cords. "And put a little of that hot sauce on it—I feel like living dangerously."

THOM T. CAUGHT UP with Trey behind the chutes. "What the hell's wrong with you, boy?" the old man griped. "You coulda been killed."

"Nah," Trey disagreed modestly. "I've rolled more cars than you can shake a stick at." *He was starting to talk like the locals!* "I knew what I was doing," he added gruffly, touched in spite of himself by the old man's concern.

Thom T. guffawed. "I ain't talkin' about the car, I'm talkin' about that chili. Oohh-ee! That stuff'll make you chase rabbits! I don't know why Texans gotta prove they got cast-iron bellies but they do—and always at some dude's expense."

He pounded Trey on an aching shoulder, laughing until tears rolled down his leathery cheeks. "Well, anyway," he said, gasping for breath, "I could put these good people wise but I ain't gonna. No, sirree-bob, I ain't gonna." And he walked away to join his cronies, happy, he would certainly have said himself, as a pig in mud.

Shaking his head, Trey looked around for Rachel. She'd avoided him since the chili incident. Instead he saw Dixie and Ruby walking toward him. He met them halfway, near the small wooden grandstand.

"Either of you seen Rachel?" he asked.

"No," they said in unison, just as Rachel walked around the corner behind them. He saw her stop short.

"Don't know where Rachel is, but Laddy's out behind the calf pens with his friends and a bottle," Dixie elaborated. "Those Coxes—the apples certainly aren't falling far from that tree."

Trey saw Rachel recoil; the color drained from her face. Whirling, she hurried back the way she'd come.

Completely unaware that she had inflicted a wound so casually, Dixie continued. "That boy has it in for you, in case you didn't know. You shouldn't have let him get away with pushin' you down the stairs at the Yellow Rose the other night. Some folks take that as a sign of weakness."

"Why'd you say that?" Trey inquired, thinking only of the raw pain he'd seen on Rachel's face.

Dixie frowned. "Say what?"

"About the apples and the Coxes."

"I merely meant . . ." She looked confused. "You're a stranger here so you wouldn't know, but . . ."

"I know all about the Coxes. That's no reason to put Rachel down."

"I thought we were talking about Laddy." Dixie drew herself up haughtily. "I have never put Rachel down, even when she followed family tradition by bearing a child out of wedlock. I pride myself on being broad-minded about such things. She does seem to have led an exemplary life since."

"And you've been watching, not to mention waiting." He glared at the social arbiter of Showdown, Texas. "Dixie, you're a snob."

Angry color suffused her face. "I don't have to stand here and be insulted," she said coldly, "certainly not when everyone in town knows of your . . . personal interest in Rachel Cox. Come, Ruby."

Dixie stalked away, back straight. Ruby stared at Trey with an expression of wary respect. "Don't believe anybody ever called her that before—to her face, anyhow."

"I'm honored to be the first." He jerked his chin toward the stands. "Rachel heard part of that."

"Ahh, too bad." Ruby looked genuinely sorry. "She's made a mistake or two, but who ain't?" She took a step after her friend, then stopped. "You know, everybody in town likes Rachel," she said in a musing tone.

"Even Dixie?"

"Even Dixie," Ruby said stoutly. "It took her longer to come around, but Rachel's a fine, upstandin' citizen and a good mama to that boy."

"Then why does Rachel seem to think she's the town leper?" Trey demanded.

Ruby sighed. "Small towns, Trey Smith, small towns. You don't know what that girl's overcome."

"Maybe." Or maybe he knew more than was good for him.

Ruby suddenly grinned. "What Rachel needs is what every woman needs—a good man. As we all know, even one of them is hard to find. Hard . . . but not impossible."

Giving Trey a quick wink, she took off after Dixie Baker.

And Trey took off after Rachel Cox, although with some reluctance. Ruby's "good man" crack made him nervous, especially coming hot on the heels of Dixie's implication that the town was already gossiping. He didn't care what they said about him, but Rachel would care too much.

By the time he found her, perched on the top row of the bleachers with Jason beside her, Trey was in no mood to mince words. "You heard what Dixie said," he announced.

She lifted her chin. "I don't know what you're talking about." Turning to her son she asked, "Will you find

Thom T. for me, honey, and see if he's ready to go back to the ranch?"

"Sure." Glancing curiously at Trey, the boy took off on his errand.

She looked after him for a moment, her face pensive. "Yes, I heard," she said. "Every so often I need to be reminded to try harder."

Trey stared at her. "Lady, you're nuts. You're practically a plaster saint now."

She laughed wryly. "You, of all people, know that's not true."

She looked so vulnerable that Trey felt something stir deep inside him—a profound tenderness completely new to him. He wanted to take her into his arms and protect her from the Dixie Bakers of this world, and the unfamiliar desire confused him. Confusion, in turn, made him angry. "Jeez, Rachel, you're harder on yourself than the people in this town could ever think of being. Lighten up, why don't you?"

She looked as if he'd slapped her. Damn, he'd meant to be supportive. So much for good intentions. "Ah, Rachel," he began.

She stood up, brushing off her slacks and looking past him toward the foot of the bleachers, where Jason, Thom T., Laddy, Virge and a host of others were assembling. There was nothing for it but to follow her down.

Laddy's crocodile smile met with a chilly scowl from Trey, but the boy seemed unfazed. "You know," he said in a jocular tone, "me 'n' the boys been talkin' and we've just about decided you may fit in around here, after all. We're ready to bury the hatchet."

"What hatchet?" Trey had no intention of making things easy for the little weasel.

Laddy licked his lips. "Just a figure of speech. Now that you're officially one a th' boys, how'd you like to come along on a little huntin' trip we got planned?" He glanced around for support, which was forthcoming from Virgil and the Partridge twins. "You ever done much huntin'?"

"Only in singles bars." What were they up to now? Planning to shoot him in the back? "What're you after? Deer? Quail? Bear?"

The knowing smiles bloomed; apparently everybody was in on the joke even before Laddy replied. "Snipe. We're goin' on a snipe hunt."

WEDNESDAY, the night of the great snipe hunt, Rachel paced restlessly around the ranch house until Thom T. took her aside and gave her what for.

"If there was ever a fella who could take care of hisself, Trey Smith is it," the old man declared. "They're just havin' a little fun with him. Let it be, Rachel."

She wanted to but couldn't. There'd been a cruel edge to Laddy's expression when they departed, an edge she didn't like. And they'd taken several coolers of beer along with the requisite gunnysacks and sticks.

Trey was on to them; she was sure of it one minute, equally sure the next that he wasn't. He showed no reluctance when they left at dusk, several pickups full of rowdy men and boys. Jason watched with a slightly wistful smile, then took a book and went to his room.

Sleep would be impossible until Rachel knew how Laddy's harebrained practical joke turned out, so she'd decided she might as well get some work done. The sooner she figured out who Trey really was, the sooner she could go back home and forget she'd ever heard of him.

She was growing more certain everyday the Yankee wasn't a Taggart. The Taggarts were all Westerners; there wasn't one of them who'd be caught east of the Mississippi on a permanent basis.

She'd discovered a definite gap in the documentation, which stretched back to Jesse Daniel Taggart, born in 1821, died in 1888. He and his wife, Nancy, had produced two children: James, the forebear of the present-day Taggarts of Showdown; and Rose, the woman whose exploits were at the heart of Showdown Days.

Rachel had finally admitted to herself that what Jesse had told her was true. Rose had indeed run away with the gunfighter Boone and not the noble Sheriff Jack. There seemed no possible way to doubt that after examining and organizing the first part of the material.

Rose and Boone had settled in California, apparently to escape his reputation and whatever he'd done to earn it. There he'd chosen to be known as Jeb, a nickname taken from the initials of his given names, Jeremy Edward Boone, and had eventually been elected to the state legislature. Boone and Rose had become the parents of four children: three girls about whom nothing further had been uncovered, and one son: John Taggart Smith, called Jack.

In 1889, Boone and Rose had run into her brother James and his wife, Diana, at the San Francisco Opera. After a splendid reunion, the two couples had apparently agreed that it would not be safe to reunite the family, since Boone was presumed dead in Showdown. In the file however, was one slightly cryptic letter Rose had written to Diana, a letter that would make sense only to those who knew the family background. She'd signed it *Mrs. Jeb Smith*.

After that, the trail grew murky. Rose's son Jack Smith had married and had two sons: Boone, born in 1906, and Thomas Taggart, born in 1910. Thomas Taggart, who'd been called "T.T.," had married a woman named Barbara about 1935 and they had also named their son John.

That son would have grown up to be Trey's father, if Trey was indeed a product of the Taggart line. But John Smith had been born in New Orleans, Louisiana, and died there in 1975. Unless some other bit of evidence lay buried in the materials yet unexplored, Rachel would have to assume he'd spent his life there, as well.

Wearily she pushed everything aside. She almost wished she could prove Trey *was* who Thom T. wanted him to be, but that wouldn't happen. Trey was sexy and exciting and sometimes charming and amusing. A Taggart he wasn't.

She only needed to look at the recurrence of Taggart names over the years—Jesse, Daniel, Boone, Taggart itself—in the Smith line. There wasn't a Trey to be found anywhere.

Glancing at the grandfather clock, she realized it was after one in the morning. What on earth did Laddy and his friends think they were doing?

As if on cue, tires crunched outside. Walking to the front door, Rachel opened it, just in time to see a disheveled Laddy bound out of a pickup. She didn't like his quick, restless energy, which should have been long since worn down.

"What is it?" she called before he even reached her. "Where's Trey?"

"Damned if I know," Laddy shot back. He halted at the foot of the steps and raked a hand through his hair. "We lost the son of a bitch somewhere in Diablo Canyon."

8

EVERYTHING was going along just fine, Laddy said, and Virge and the Partridge twins backed him up on that. They'd explained the game plan to Trey, who'd agreed that as a newcomer to the "sport" of snipe hunting, he should have the honor of holding the gunnysack open while the others flushed out the pesky critters and ran 'em into the trap.

The "hunters" had set off, beating the brush with sticks and yelling, "Snipe! Snipe!" while Trey hunched over an open burlap bag waving a large flashlight to attract the little creatures.

Only they'd been moving away from him, not toward him, back to the trucks and the coolers of beer. Then, when they'd sneaked back hours later to enjoy their victim's humiliation, he was gone.

"Well, where in tarnation did you leave him?" Thom T. demanded. The commotion had awakened the old man and he wasn't in the best of moods. He didn't seem concerned about Trey so much as mad over losing sleep.

Laddy shuffled his feet and looked uncomfortable. "Over near Diablo Canyon," he admitted. "But he wouldn't be dumb enough to wander in there, would he?"

"If he did he's a goner," Virgil announced.

Thom T. shrugged. "It's possible. There's more gullies and washes and dead ends in there than you can shake a stick at." He turned to leave. "Yawl done it, yawl figger it out. But do it quiet and let a' old man get some shut-eye."

Rachel turned on her brother, so angry she could barely keep her hands from his throat. "This is your idea of getting even, Laddy Cox, but all you've succeeded in doing is making a fool out of yourself!"

His face reddened. "That's not fair. Anything happens to him, it's his own fault."

"Really?" Her scorn scalded him. "Like it was his fault he fell off the balcony at the Yellow Rose? Like it was his fault the stupid brakes went out on your car? Sure, Laddy, it's his fault—his fault for telling the truth about you!"

She gasped and pressed one hand over her mouth. She hadn't meant to say that; didn't, in fact, believe it. Trey was wrong about Laddy, but all the dangerous practical jokes had made her lose her temper.

Before she could apologize, Virge stuck in his two cents' worth. "She ain't just a-whistlin' Dixie, Lad. You been eatin' crow since you locked horns with this dude."

"Damn straight," Shayne Partridge agreed. "This Yankee's a ring-tailed snorter. He's took ever'thing you could throw at him and keeps comin' back for more." He exchanged a significant look with his twin. "Until now. Now he's prob'ly dead at the foot of Diablo Falls."

Rachel's stomach knotted. What if Shayne was right? She swung on her brother, but he wasn't waiting around for another tongue-lashing.

"If that's how yawl feel . . ." Laddy clenched his fists in impotent fury. Whirling, he ran out of the house. They heard a pickup start and tires screech as he tore out of the ranch yard.

Dwayne, Shayne and Virge exchanged blank looks. "Well," Virge said uncomfortably, "I guess we'd best get on home and let you get some sleep, Rachel."

"Sleep! When a man could be wandering around in Diablo Canyon lost or hurt?"

The three young men shrugged. "Or dead," Dwayne added helpfully.

"Look at the bright side," Virge suggested. "He coulda found the back way out. That path over the north rim empties out not two miles from here."

"A 'course, he'd a' had to be part mountain goat to climb up a strange canyon wall in the dark without breakin' his neck," Shayne said. "But hell, he could be pert-near home by now."

"Even if he ain't there's nothin' to be done till daylight," Dwayne added. "We'll be back when we can see what we're doin'."

Alone, Rachel wondered how this situation had gotten so completely out of hand. Sensing movement in the doorway, she turned. Jason stood there, rubbing sleep from his eyes.

"Don't worry, Mom." He walked over and gave her a hug. "I got a hunch Virge is right."

Her son had returned to bed before she even remembered what Virge had said. *He coulda found the back way out.*

From his vantage point atop the hill between the big house and the smaller foreman's quarters where he was living, Trey saw Laddy rush out, jump into a pickup and roar away. A few minutes later, the trio he'd named Three Stooges followed more slowly.

Fifteen minutes after that, Rachel came outside and hesitated, looking around. Trey lay on his belly on a sleeping bag and watched her. He was much too far away to see her expression, although after a dark and starless beginning, the night was now clear and silvery.

And warm, hot, really. He'd worked up a sweat climbing out over the back wall of the canyon, then jogging home. He'd grabbed a sleeping bag and carried it up this hill in case the mighty snipe hunters came looking for him—which they did, their racket waking him from peaceful slumber beneath the stars.

He'd watched with amusement as they piled out of their vehicles like Keystone Kops to swarm into the foreman's house. Finding nothing, they loaded up again and roared away, proving once again that in a battle of wits, Laddy and his buddies were only half-armed.

Trey would have liked to be a fly on the wall when they told Rachel what they'd done. She'd know, even if Laddy didn't, that Trey had been damned generous thus far. The kid'd been asking for it; Trey could have found any number of ways and means to let him have it.

Was she wondering why he hadn't? Or had she figured that out, too? If she hadn't, it was time—hell, past time—for him to come clean about his profession. She'd see the humor in the situation, he hoped. And once past that initial hurdle, he could deal with the next. Would he be able to convince Rachel her secret was safe with him?

Below, the shadow that was Rachel walked to a car parked in the driveway beside the house. Trey raised himself higher on his elbows to watch. Where the hell was she going? It must be 2:00 a.m.

If she turned toward town, it would probably be to get the sheriff. In that event, Trey figured he ought to head her off and confess on the spot.

Or she might drive up this hill to see if somehow he'd found his way out of the canyon. If she did that . . . he scooted back on his belly, away from the lookout's edge. Flopping onto his back, he stared at stars so bright and near he was tempted to pluck a handful to fling at her feet.

His throat closed up and desire surged through him. His pulse thrummed so strongly that he fancied he felt an answering heartbeat in the warm earth upon which he lay.

He still hadn't recovered from his generosity the other night. Damn, he wanted her. After holding her in his arms, kissing her, touching her, being singed by her inner fires, he no longer cared if she came to him as the uptight Rachel or the freewheeling Liz. He'd take her any way he could get her and be damn grateful.

Just once; twice if he liked it. His mouth stretched into a tight smile. Love 'em and leave 'em, preferably asking for more. His freedom and independence weren't at stake here, he assured himself. His sanity . . . maybe.

The sudden rumble of an automobile pierced the quiet night. Trey's every muscle clenched. Which way would she choose?

His way. Damn! He'd have her alone out here in the middle of the night, emotions already running high and

memories of their last encounter adding a special edge.
And he wouldn't be so damned generous again!

His most lascivious dreams were about to come true.

RACHEL SAW a flicker of flame as she topped the rise
separating the two houses, just a tiny pinpoint of light
near the crest of the hill. Even as it registered with her,
the small fire flared higher.

It never occurred it could be anyone but Trey Smith.
Without a moment's hesitation, she turned her car off
the road and headed toward the light, weaving between trees until she suddenly realized it wasn't safe to
drive any farther. Climbing out near a clump of scrub
oak, she hurried on afoot.

By the time she reached the summit she was winded.
She stepped into the circle of light and bent forward,
gasping for breath.

Trey lay stretched on a sleeping bag beside a cheery
fire, a fire he couldn't possibly need for warmth in this
heat and humidity.

"Are you all right?" she gasped.

He looked surprised. "Never better. You?"

Groaning, she straightened. "I've got a stitch in my
side," she complained, looking around for some place
to sit. "You sure you're okay? Honestly, Trey, you scared
the—"

He patted his sleeping bag. "Sit here," he invited.

She shouldn't; it was the spider and the fly all over
again. She knew she shouldn't get anywhere near him,
but she did. Holding her side, she sank onto the far-
thest corner of the sleeping bag and sucked in a quivering breath before facing him.

"Want to tell me how you got here?" she challenged.

"Walked."

"Up the side of Diablo Canyon? In the dark?"

He grinned. The firelight shadowing his lean cheeks gave his features an appropriately devilish cast. "Okay, I mostly climbed."

"But…" Staring at him, she noticed for the first time that the only thing he wore was a pair of soft blue Levi's. The broad chest with its mat of black hair rippled in the golden glow of the firelight, turning him into some mythic hero capable of all kinds of superhuman feats.

Like those he'd already performed: tumbling down a flight of stairs, rolling a car, escaping from a dangerous canyon in the dead of night.

Making love to her and making her like it. "You weren't lost," she said, suddenly sure.

He cocked his head to one side. "Nope."

"You . . . could you possibly have rolled Laddy's car on purpose?"

"Yep." His lips twisted with what looked like suppressed humor.

"And I'll just bet those stairs at the Yellow Rose weren't the first you ever fell down."

"That's right."

"Trey Smith, who are you, some kind of superman?"

He laughed. "Not hardly." He achieved a fair approximation of a Texas drawl. "What I am is a Hollywood stuntman, darlin'."

"Why, why—you jerk!" While she was worrying about him, he'd been playing them all for fools. She shouldn't have wasted a single sympathetic thought on him. She shouldn't care *what* happened to him.

But even as she sputtered in outrage, she was remembering how neatly he'd turned the tables on Laddy and his friends. They'd set out to humiliate and embarrass the damn Yankee, and instead they'd made themselves the laughingstock of Jones County.

It served them right. She began to smile, twisting quickly away so he wouldn't see. "You don't play fair," she accused, aware that her voice sounded strangled.

"It's not my game," he reminded her.

"That's true." She swallowed hard. "D-did—?" She choked off the rest of the question, dipping her chin and pressing her lips together to keep from collapsing into helpless laughter.

"Are you crying?"

He sounded utterly appalled by that possibility. She felt his hands on her shoulders, his touch shredding the last of her restraint.

"Are you crying?" he repeated, his voice under pressure now.

The more she thought about it, the funnier it got. Her shoulders shook, and something very near hysteria rose into her throat. Speaking took maximum effort. "I'm not crying."

She collapsed into his arms, laughing so hard that tears ran down her cheeks.

TREY LAUGHED WITH HER, but his heart wasn't in it. The feel of her, soft and tempting in his arms, was his undoing. Even while he pretended to enjoy the joke, he was shifting, moving to bring her more fully against his aroused body.

At the first opportunity he rolled onto his back once more, taking her with him. As abruptly as it had begun, her laughter ceased.

She said his name, a little catch in her voice: "Trey?"

He heard the question that really wasn't one. She knew what was happening. He pressed his hips against her taut belly, wanting there to be no doubt at all. Her breath caught on a hungry little moan.

"The other night..." She seemed unable to go on, nor did she protest when he fumbled at the buttons on her shirt.

"The other night was only a preview," he promised, opening her shirt. Damn, she wasn't wearing a bra. She must have dressed in a hurry to come looking for him. Uttering a choked exclamation, he slid down to take the tip of one breast into his mouth and swirl his tongue around the turgid nipple.

"A . . . a preview?" Her languid sigh preceded a general loosening of her body, as if she'd decided in that instant to forego all pretense. "You were . . . so generous then. . . ."

He lifted his head, tugging lightly at her nipple before releasing it. "I won't be again," he warned, his hands covering the soft mounds of her breasts with a circular kneading motion. As her agitation increased, she pressed closer to him. "I couldn't be, even if I wanted to. Because you, my little librarian . . ."

He slipped his hands around her ribs, lifting her torso. Her breasts stood out in pale splendor and he buried his face between them. "You, my duplicitous darling, have been driving me out of my mind."

"M-me?"

He heard her genuine surprise, coupled with a rising wonder. What the hell was the matter with Texas men? Hadn't any of them seen past the ladylike exterior to the latent sensuality burning inside this woman?

"Yes, you." He kissed his way down her midriff to the button of her slacks, which he dispatched with dexterity. He thrust his tongue into her belly button and she convulsed.

He slid his hand down her belly beneath her clothing to curve his fingers between her thighs; she groaned and let him nudge her legs apart. She wasn't going to fight this; what was more important, she wasn't going to fight herself. His blood roaring in his ears, he felt her hands clutch at his shoulders and almost lost it there and then.

Too damned long. It'd been too damned long since he'd made love. The intensity of his arousal shocked him; he was about to explode and knew it. His best efforts at control weren't going to be enough to delay the short time fuse he was on.

He wanted to slow down but it was no use. *Why try?* he asked himself, savoring the wet heat between her thighs. She was ready, he was ready. . . .

But he'd be damned if he'd take her with both of them half-dressed and clawing at each other like wildcats. First the clothes, then . . .

"I'm sorry," he whispered into her ear. "I wanted to take my time, but . . ."

He wasn't sure she'd even heard him over the rasp of his heavy breathing until she groaned. "Not slow, fast. *Now!*"

She rose to meet his first powerful stroke, her hands on his buttocks guiding him into her throbbing depths.

Her tightness startled him and he hesitated, breath scorching his lungs. Grabbing the initiative, she wrapped her slender legs more tightly around him, drawing him deep, deep, deeper into her eager heat.

The delirium of their union shocked him a little, but fierce pleasure quickly overwhelmed all else. Unleashed now, she clutched at him, even scraping her nails down his back when her orgasm overtook her. She cried out, tightening around him like a velvet fist. He arched back, straining to prolong her pleasure before taking his own, completely forgetting his vow to think first of his own fulfillment.

But it was impossible to deny himself for long. His body clenched, then exploded into a climax more powerful than any he'd felt before. A melting weakness invaded every muscle, and he gathered her close, holding her as if he'd never let her go.

RACHEL STARED BLANKLY into what was left of the bonfire, a few glowing coals and ashes. She lay on her side, cuddled back to front in Trey's arms. With one hand he idly caressed her left breast.

Body languid with satisfaction, mind overwhelmed by the enormity of what had just happened, she struggled to find her way back to reality.

Because, of course, this was not reality and never could be. She had a son to think about, a reputation and a position in this community. She wouldn't jeopardize all that, even for him.

Since she obviously couldn't trust herself to resist him, she had no choice but to avoid him from here on. That was the obvious solution, but still she worried over the problem, desperate for another answer.

He leaned closer and she felt the pressure of his muscular chest against her shoulder blades. His breath tickled the tendrils of hair escaping from her braid. At the moist flick of his tongue, she quivered like a doe caught in a spotlight.

"Wow." He nuzzled her ear. "I never thought..." He sounded almost self-conscious when he cleared his throat. "What have you done to me, sweetheart?" He smoothed back her hair and kissed her temple. "Baby..." He nipped her earlobe. "Liz..." His tongue flicked out to touch her throat. "Rachel, love..." He maneuvered her onto her back, his hands cupping her breasts.

His low croon quickened her pulse; his every touch sent shivers down her spine—until she realized what he had said. *Liz?* "Wh-what did you call me?" she demanded.

"Wonderful. Because you are. You're also beautiful...." With one hand he plucked at a rigid nipple. "And sexy." He slid the other hand down her stomach to bury his fingers between her thighs.

All kinds of urgent sensations flooded through her body, but her mind was suddenly as cold and clear as glass. "Liz," she said numbly. "You called me Liz."

"Liz—darling, sweetheart, baby." He smiled at her through the moonlight's silver glow. "You know what they say about a rose by any other name."

He leaned over her raised breasts, his head blocking out the full moon. Nuzzling the sensitive undercurves, he flicked his quick tongue, first across one nipple, then the other. Rachel whimpered, feeling a tingle all the way to the soles of her feet. She never wanted him to stop; she'd never felt more alive ... more complete.

He insinuated his hand more deeply between her trembling thighs, and her determination wavered. She would not surrender again to the wild rapture of his lovemaking—or maybe she would, just one more time. . . .

"No!" *Laddy wasn't the only one Trey was making a fool of.* With her last shred of self-possession, she rolled away and sat up. Grabbing her crushed clothing off the ground, she clutched it to her breast and took a deep, painful breath.

He leaned over and caught her arm. "What the hell?" He sounded astonished. "Did I do something you didn't like?"

"You called me Liz." She stood up and yanked on her slacks, fumbling with the button. She trembled so badly she finally gave up, depending on the zipper to keep everything in place.

"Liz." Trey sat up, shoving back his dark hair with both hands. "I've heard of guys getting in trouble for saying the wrong name but never the *right* one. That's your name, isn't it, Rachel Elizabeth?"

So he was going to brazen it out. She offered a short, sharp, scornful sound and dragged on the blouse. "Sure, only you weren't supposed to know. How'd you find out?"

"I didn't find out. The starchy librarian fooled me for a couple of minutes, but I put two and two together the first time I went to your house and saw you with Laddy. Jason had already told me your nickname was Liz."

"You got my son involved in this?"

He frowned as if finally aware of how angry she was. "What's the big deal? You played a trick on me at the

Alamo Cantina and I paid you back. I'd say we're even."

"*Even!* How can we be even? You've got nothing to lose." Panting, she faced him, her blouse hanging unbuttoned while her hands clenched.

"But—"

"Shut up and listen." She closed her eyes for a moment to gather her thoughts, her strength. "I didn't disguise myself and go to the Alamo to fool *you*, I did it to protect *me*— my reputation and my family. It's not as if I dress up and cruise bars in my spare time, for heaven's sake. But I've got a lot to live down in this town and I can't do it by barhopping, even if it is only to drag my brother home."

"A lot to live down," he repeated slowly. "Such as?"

"Such as getting pregnant when I was barely sixteen."

He made a faintly disparaging sound. "Big deal. It happens all the time, even to the nicest girls."

"Ah," she said bitterly, "I see you've already heard. Well, for your information, it was a long time ago, and I wasn't one of the nicest girls. I was one of the trashy Cox girls."

"I can relate. I didn't exactly grow up palling around with the Kennedys myself."

"No, you can't relate! For one thing, you just don't know small towns." She shook her head sharply. "For another, you're a man. Your reputation's enhanced by the kind of thing that ruins a woman."

"Why didn't you leave, then? You didn't have to hang around and take the abuse."

She glared at him. "This is home. My family has lived here for generations—on the wrong side of the figurative tracks, but they've been here. I guess I wanted to show everybody that a Cox can be just as good as—as a Baker or a Taggart or anybody else."

"Where was Jason's father while all this was going on?" Trey grabbed his Levi's and stood up to pull them on.

"Jason..." Rachel licked dry lips. "Jason's father never knew anything about it. He...died before I could even tell him I was pregnant."

Trey paused, his hand on the zipper of his fly. "Did you love each other?" he asked in a flat voice.

"Love?" She shrugged helplessly. "I thought so, but it was so long ago that I can hardly remember. Maybe I was just in love with love. I don't know whether he'd have married me or not."

Trey pulled up his zipper. "So we all make mistakes."

"Yes, and if we're smart we learn from them. There's no way that's ever going to happen to me again."

He looked affronted. "I'm from California, for Chris' sake. We know about condoms." His voice grew softer. "So you stayed right here in Showdown, had your baby and kept him. That was gutsy, Rachel."

"It was stupid." She raked her fingers through her hair. "I shouldn't have. I was just a kid myself. I had plans. Everybody told me the baby would be better off with two loving parents, but I just—I just couldn't give him up. Because..." Her voice grew soft. "He was all I had and I loved him, from the very first moment I knew I was pregnant."

She looked at Trey, feeling intensely vulnerable but unable to stop the words tumbling out. "Even when I had to work two jobs and skip meals myself to feed him,

I wasn't sorry I kept my son. Because everybody needs love, Trey Smith...."

"Not really." His tone changed, grew hard and cold. "You didn't need to please anybody except yourself, Rachel. Your mistake was in caring too much. If you don't care, the bastards can't get you."

"But I did care. I still do. At first I thought it was only for Jason's sake, but it's more than that. The Coxes have never been anything in this town, and I guess I'm hungry for respectability, for myself and my son and my brother. That's why, when I've occasionally had to pull Laddy out of bars, I've ... well, I haven't wanted anyone to know. I don't want to be seen in places like that or associated with them. It's just too much to deal with."

She bit her lip, remembering the times she'd begged her father to come home from whatever bar he happened to be in.

Trey flexed his shoulder muscles, speaking impatiently. "Rachel, you're only human. Anyone expecting more of you than that isn't being realistic—including you. There's a sexy, passionate woman inside there screaming to get out."

She lifted her chin defensively. "All the Coxes have a wild streak. Nobody knows that better than I do. It just means I have to be twice as careful and twice as good as anybody else in this town. I can handle it—at least I could before *you* came along."

"My point exactly."

He caught her by the waist and stepped close. She shivered and hunched her shoulders against his dangerous appeal.

"It's no good," she said. "You've had your fun. You've pried out all my secrets."

"Except one. Who's Jason's father, Rachel?"

"That's none of your business." She looked away, her cheek brushing against his chest. "Why don't you leave me alone? I don't even know who you are, not really. We may never know for sure."

She shoved away from him and stepped back into the shadows. "Find somebody else to play with while you're in Texas. Because I'm not going to put everything I've worked for in jeopardy for a quick lay—no matter how good it is."

TREY HAD HEARD; he simply did not understand or accept.

This was the nineties, for Chris'sake. She'd done nothing to be ashamed of, nothing except whet his appetite and then walk away.

He was good and mad and yet . . .

Somehow she had managed to stir him—him, hard as nails, independent Trey Smith. He'd become emotionally involved with a woman for the first time in a very long time and he didn't like it one damned bit.

Time to heed his own advice.

If you don't care, nobody can get you. *Yeah, remember that, Smith.*

TREY SMITH faced Laddy Cox across Thom T.'s breakfast table, his anger so white-hot that he saw the boy recoil before it. Trey didn't know where the hell Jason was but was glad he wouldn't witness this.

"I'm tired of messing with you, kid," Trey snarled. "Next time you come at me you're gonna get more than you bargained for. Understand?"

"It was all a joke," Laddy retorted. "Nobody got hurt."

"Yeah, and ain't that a wonder." Trey spat out the words. "I'm fed up with teaching you the same lesson over and over again, so I'm telling you flat out—back off."

Laddy stuck out his jaw. "Or what?"

"Or..." Trey leaned forward and whispered into Laddy's ear; sitting back, he saw that the kid's face had gone white.

"You wouldn't—dammit, you couldn't!"

Thom T. slammed down his spoon. "Don't know what he told you, boy, but I'm willin' to bet he not only can but will if you push him."

Laddy swung to his sister for support. "Rachel?"

Filled with guilt at the pleasure she had savored last night in Trey's arms, she felt her face flush at Laddy's appeal.

"Yeah, *Rachel.*" Trey's tone dripped sarcasm. "Jump in here and save your brother's butt one more time."

"Be reasonable, Trey," she pleaded. "Laddy didn't mean any harm."

Trey straightened and gave her a scathing look. "If you'll lie about one thing, you'll lie about another," he said. "That does it. I'm washing my hands of the whole Cox family. You can all go to hell. It's none of my business."

Rachel buried her face in her shaking hands until the sound of his angry footsteps had faded. Then she looked at Thom T. "If that man's a Taggart, I'm Mary

Queen of Scots!" she cried. "I can't take this anymore. Jason and I are moving back to town."

Thom T. shook his head stubbornly. "I need you here," he said. "As a personal favor, I gotta ask you to keep diggin'."

9

TREY KNEW what he wanted to do, but for the first time in his life, didn't know how to go about doing it. He wanted out—out of Showdown, out of Texas. But he didn't want to hurt Thom T. in the process.

Jesse called a week or so after the snipe hunt and Trey let loose. "Man, I'm going bonkers around here!" he stormed. "I need to get back to the bright lights and the big city."

"Can't you hold out a tad longer?" Jesse sounded harassed, as if he'd already had an argument or two about this with his grandfather. "Thom T. says another batch of stuff is on its way from that detective's widow. Rachel's got just about everything worked out now, up to the very last generation. If you'll be patient a little longer..."

"Dammit, I don't want some dead detective telling me I'm a Taggart when I know I'm not. I've sponged off the old boy long enough."

A disparaging sound came over the wire. "Grandpa says you've been doin' the work of two men on the ranch, not to mention keepin' him company and givin' Rachel's boy the kind of attention he's been needin'. Grandpa says he's gonna start payin' you—"

"No way, man. I came here to get well. I'm well. I'm tired of dickin' around with this. I want to get the hell back to my own life."

Trey was still brooding two days later as he drove Thom T. and Jason into town; pissed because he was still in Texas, and because the longer he stayed, the harder it was going to be to go. Hell, he hadn't even tried to bring up the subject of leaving with the old man, he thought with disgust.

He pulled to the curb before the hardware store to drop off his two passengers. Then he planned to head on to San Antonio, for no other reason than to combat cabin fever. The old man and the boy would meet Rachel at the library in a couple of hours for the ride back to the ranch; Trey would return in a day or two.

Unless he could think of a plausible reason not to.

"How about a cupa coffee before you hit the road?" Thom T. invited, holding the car door open.

"Sure." Trey had agreed before he could talk himself out of the chance he'd ostensibly been waiting for. "There's something I've been meaning to talk to you about, anyway."

Jason jumped out of the car. "I think I'll go get an ice-cream cone." He glanced at Thom T. "I'll meet you and Mom at the library at five."

Trey blocked the boy's path. "Got any money?" Now why the hell did he ask? Trey berated himself. *Kid's not my responsibility.*

Jason grinned that wide-eyed, eager grin. "I'll get some from Mom."

"Ah, don't bother her." Trey pulled out a handful of coins and offered them. After a moment's hesitation, Jason cupped his hands to accept the largess.

Trey stood there for a moment, watching the boy amble down the street, a book under his arm. There went a nice kid. A damned nice kid.

With a damned difficult mother.

He followed Thom T. into the hardware store, past counters piled high with merchandise. With a friendly wave to the proprietor, the old man led the way to the back of the store, where the coffeepot never ran dry.

"So what's on your mind?" Thom T. asked, blowing on the contents of his cup to cool it.

"Leaving. That's what's on my mind." No use trying to sugarcoat it.

Thom T. got that stubborn glint in his eyes. "Rachel ain't figgered things out yet. What's your hurry?"

"Man, I'm going stir-crazy." Trey felt as if his eyes must be bulging like a wild man's, so deeply did he mean what he was saying. "I gotta get the hell out of here."

Thom T. frowned. Suddenly he gave a snort of laughter. "I know what your problem is, son. You need to get your ashes hauled."

"I need—what?" Trey stared at the old man, dumb-founded. "Why, you old . . . dog!"

"Shocked you, did I? You young folks think yawl invented it, but I'm here to tell you that in my day . . ." He rolled his eyes and grinned. "Didn't find your Lizzie, I take it. Too bad—maybe you can fix what's ailin' you in San Antone."

Trey gripped the plastic foam cup so tightly that it buckled, splashing hot coffee over his arm and wrist. "No way. It's not healthy to sleep with strangers, you old coot."

Thom T.'s grin grew wider. "I thought a' that," he said smugly. "Here, I got somethin' for you." He reached into his pocket and pulled out a small package. "Johnny over to th' drugstore almost had a heart attack when I bought 'em and I didn't tell him no different. Hell, he's seventy if he's a day—it give him hope."

Trey stared down at a box of condoms, then back up at the eighty-something gentleman who'd offered them. "Is nothing sacred?" he asked.

"These days? Not a danged thang," Thom T. said complacently. "It'd be a better world if folks'd just say no, but you cain't lock the barn door after the horse's been stole, know what I mean?" He nudged Trey with an elbow. "I thought there for a while you and Sissy was gettin'... friendly. What went wrong?"

"I'm not gonna stand here in the middle of a hardware store in some nowhere town in Texas and discuss my sex life with a guy old enough to be my grandfather," Trey declared.

"I practic'ly am your grandpa, boy," Thom T. scoffed.

"The hell you are!" Because he didn't know what else to do with them, Trey thrust the condoms into his pocket.

"Gotta say my piece." The old man looked suddenly serious. "I've come to love you just like Jesse and Boone. We're family, and you're in my will right alongside 'em. There ain't nothin' you cain't talk to me about, and that includes your..." He glanced around surreptitiously, then whispered, "sex life."

Trey stared at the old man. *"We're not family,"* he said past tight jaws. "I don't have any family and never did—and I sure as hell don't want to be in your will. Damnation, I already told you that! No wonder she thinks I'm a fortune hunter!" Tossing the crumpled cup into a nearby trash can, he bolted for the front door.

Running, he thought, *just like you always do when the going gets tough.*

Damn, he didn't want to care about Thom T. Taggart or anybody else in this hick town. Especially not a certain complicated woman who had a way of making him forget everything except how much he wanted her.

Driving out of town, he spotted Jason. The boy stood in front of the Dairy Domicile, licking a big Curly-Qs cone and smiling shyly at Dixie Baker.

Trey realized his troubles were multiplying. Because sure as death and taxes, Jason's father was Dixie's dead son Bobby. Rachel was depriving her son of his grandmother and Dixie of her grandson.

It wasn't fair.

It wasn't right.

And somebody ought by God to *do* something about that. Maybe somebody who knew what it was to grow up an outsider.

What the hell? The library was on the way out of town. Practically.

Trey turned right at the next corner, meeting another vehicle in the intersection. He didn't recognize the car, but he sure as hell knew the driver.

Laddy flipped up one finger of the hand holding the bottle of beer, then laid rubber out of there.

"OR I'LL HUFF and I'll puff and I'll blow your house down!" Rachel sat on a low chair in the middle of a half circle of children, holding a large picture book on her lap. "What would you do if you were a little piggy and the mean old wolf was at the door?" she asked her enchanted audience.

The children shouted out their answers? "I'd hit that old wolf in the nose!" "I'd hide under the bed?" And from Debbie Sue Greenleaf, "I'd cry!"

Trey grinned. Debbie Sue would cry, con the other two little piggies into facing the big bad wolf, then sneak out the back door before the roof fell in. The kid didn't miss a trick.

Rachel began to read again, and he just stood there, drinking in the sight and sound. She wore a dress of some sky-blue material, the full skirt falling around her in graceful folds. And her hair... Instead of being slicked back tightly, it was contained in a loose bun on top of her head, tendrils escaping to curl around her nape and face.

God, she was beautiful, he thought; neither Rachel nor Liz but the best parts of each. A whole person in her own right, if she'd only let it happen. He wanted to sweep her into his arms and carry her away.

Damn! He had come in anger, determined to force the issue of Jason's father for the boy's sake, and to confront her with Laddy's drinking for the hell of it. Trey knew he had nothing to lose where Rachel was concerned, for she'd hardly given him the time of day since he'd slipped and called her Liz.

So why couldn't he maintain the anger? He'd spent a lot of frustrated hours trying—and failing—to figure out what made her so different from the other women he'd bedded. Yet different she was. Even looking at her in the middle of a gang of crumb snatchers gave him a raging hard-on.

"And the three little pigs lived happily ever after." Rachel closed the book, impervious to pleas for more.

Smiling parents moved in to claim their offspring. Rachel smiled, too, until she looked up and saw Trey.

She started visibly and an almost haunted expression crossed her face. But she didn't try to avoid him. As if she could, he thought, moving with care to circumvent the little people swarming between them. Rachel waited, her gaze level and determined.

To cover his anxiety, Trey spoke abruptly. "I need to talk to you."

"About—?" Her dark brows rose.

"It's personal."

"In that case, no. I don't have time for personal conversations when I'm working." She carried the picture book to a shelf, checked the books already there, then slid it into its proper place.

That was Rachel; a place for everything and everything in its place. Unfortunately, she had no place in her life for Trey or any other man, apparently. When she turned and found him still standing there, she frowned. "I thought you were on your way to San Antone."

"I was. I mean, I am."

"Then don't let me keep you."

When she would have walked past, he stepped into her path. "So we're back to the virgin queen routine," he said sarcastically. "Whatever turns you on, babe. I just dropped by because your brother and your son—"

"Damn you!" She spoke in a low but passionate voice. "Will you ever quit meddling?"

"I'm not meddling, I've been suckered in." He concentrated on his anger, unwilling to deal with all the other feelings she aroused in him. "Jeez, what planet are you living on? You can't stand between Jason and Laddy and the real world forever. The road to hell is *paved* with good intentions—mostly yours."

Her chin rose another notch. "Look who's talking. You're the worst buttinsky I've ever met."

"I . . ." He started to protest, realized he didn't have a leg to stand on and substituted an embarrassed, ". . . know." he shoved one hand through his overlong hair. "What the hell's wrong with me? I never used to be this way. You're really messing with my mind, lady."

"I'm doing no such thing." She tried to step around him but he moved with her. She glanced about anxiously. "People are staring," she hissed. "There's already talk about us. Will you please *go?*"

He brightened. "What kind of talk?"

Her cheeks turned scarlet and she refused to look at him. "Apparently . . . somebody saw us kissing in the alley after you fell off the—" her eyes narrowed "—*jumped* off that balcony."

"Was brutally pushed, you mean." He grinned, feeling suddenly better. "Why don't we give them something new to talk about?"

He grabbed her shoulders, hauled her against his chest and kissed her, hard and fast. The only satisfaction he got out of it was knowing how mad she was going to be, but dammit! She needed to learn that the world wouldn't stop turning if Rachel Elizabeth Cox kicked up her heels once in a—

The crack of her palm across his cheek knocked all those smugly supercilious thoughts right out of his head, at the same time rocking him back on his heels. He stared at her in astonishment, only gradually becoming aware of a twittering behind him.

Rachel pointed toward the door. "Get out of my library!" she commanded in righteous tones. "And don't come back!"

He went, so mad that he was thirty miles down the road before he realized that he hadn't brought up either of the things he'd gone into the library to talk to her about: her son's paternity and her brother's foolhardiness.

"SHH! MIZ COX IS IN A BAD MOOD!"

Rachel stopped slamming books around and took a deep breath, struggling to compose herself. She forced a smile for Debbie Sue, whose loud whisper had been aimed at Tammy Garcia. "No, I'm not," she said. "I'll prove it. I'll take Sonny Bunny out of his cage and let you play with him."

While the two little girls ohhed and ahhed over the floppy-eared rabbit who lived in the children's library, Rachel tried to figure out why she was still so unnerved by her confrontation with Trey Smith almost an hour ago.

She couldn't even think about him without remembering the night she'd spent in his arms—a mistake, of course, an aberration in a carefully ordered life.

A beautiful, glorious mistake, one she relived over and over again. It was her secret; for a few brief hours he had shown her sensuality beyond her wildest dreams . . . and she had reveled in it.

That lapse must never be repeated; it represented a threat to everything she held dear. Or at least, everything she'd held dear before she met Trey Smith. . . .

SAN ANTONIO was a bust. The night scene looked sleazy, the women available; cheap when compared to Rachel Elizabeth Cox. Since he wasn't into booze, that left his social options somewhat limited.

He spent two days doggedly doing the tourist bit. He visited the Lone Star Brewery and the Buckhorn Hall of Horns because the waitress who served his breakfast had told him he should. He was just starting to enjoy wandering through Brackenridge Park when he saw a boy who reminded him of Jason admiring the Brackenridge Eagle, a scale model of a diesel train.

Quickly Trey turned away. This he didn't need. Nor did he need to see the young man who reminded him of Laddy, strolling along the River Walk with his arm around a pretty, dark-haired girl; or the silver-haired businessman standing at the hotel bar, holding a young couple enthralled with his stories.

His stories didn't hold a candle to Thom T.'s.

What he didn't see was anyone who reminded him of Rachel, or Liz, either. She was one of a kind, or two, depending on how you looked at it.

The only thing that made any impression on Trey was the Alamo. Standing in the courtyard of the historic mission, he readily related to the band of 187 Texas volunteers fighting to the last man against a Mexican army of thousands.

On the monument in Alamo Plaza he found the name he sought. *James Taggart.* A chill raced down his spine as he stared at the letters inscribed in marble. And as he stood there, a new and frightening feeling crept over him. What would it be like to *really* belong to the Taggart family?

Or to any family. He'd never known his father, and
his mother had died when he was six, a victim of
drugs—prescription drugs, so one of his foster mothers had told him. All he had left of them was a photograph taken on their wedding day. Shunted from one
foster home to another by the City of New York, he'd
grown up wary and independent—but he had grown
up, unlike the majority of his foster siblings and friends.

I don't want to think about this, he warned himself,
standing beneath the broiling July sun in the middle of
Alamo Plaza, cold sweat rolling down his back and his
stomach clenched in denial. He saw tourists give him
guarded glances and a wide berth. "What's wrong with
that man?" a little girl piped up before her mother
dragged her away.

What's wrong with that man? The kid's question was
valid. Instead of looking forward, that man kept looking back. Fear controlled him, and it wasn't only his
fear of needles. In fact, his most paralyzing fear was of
sharing his life.

He was afraid to count on people, afraid to let himself care. He had lost everyone he'd ever loved and he'd
learned the hard way that it just wasn't worth the risk.

But could Rachel be an exception to that rule? And
what about Thom T. and Jason? Turning his back on
the Alamo, he walked away, thinking about all the
things that could happen to people, usually—but not
always—things of their own doing.

Like Laddy. The booze would eventually get him if
he didn't wake up. And Rachel. Rigid, self-imposed re-
pression was going to cause all that beautiful, wild
passion to shrivel up and die.

Thom T. was getting old. To be honest, Thom T. *was* old. He wouldn't last forever. And Jason, young Jason, trying to grow to manhood without a father to help him . . . *like me,* Trey reflected.

So he told himself what he always told himself when he felt his resolve weaken, *Get a grip! I do all right by myself. I mind my own business and I don't stick my nose where it doesn't belong.*

That's right, I don't need them—

But they sure as hell need me, every damned one of them.

JASON RAN OUTSIDE to greet Trey on his return. Walking onto the front porch, Rachel felt a relief so great it made her knees weak. She clutched at a wooden column and tried to keep her welcoming smile within the bounds of propriety.

She'd missed him. God help her, she'd missed him something awful.

Trey dropped an arm easily around the boy's shoulders. "I brought you something," he said.

"What?" Jason's eyes sparkled with pleasure. "A book?"

"You already got one a' them," Trey teased. "Better. I brought you a football. Thought we could toss around the old pigskin— What's your problem, kid?"

Jason shuffled his feet and looked at the ground. "I'm no good at sports," he mumbled. "Laddy got me a football for Christmas a couple years ago and I'm just no good."

Rachel's heart ached for her son and she took a step forward. A quick, warning glance from Trey stopped her.

"Hey!" The man grabbed a handful of the boy's hair and tilted his head back. "Did Laddy show you how to handle the ball?"

"Well, he said he would. I mean, with his job at the service station and all . . ."

Trey felt his mouth tighten but he didn't say a word against Laddy. "I don't have a job at the moment so I've got lots of time."

Jason shook his head. "I'm just no good," he repeated.

"Listen to me, kid." Trey spoke with utter conviction. "I doubt you'll ever be drafted by the Dallas Cowboys, but I can sure as hell teach you enough to keep you from being humiliated in gym class and have fun doing it, too. If you really don't want to, say so now, because I'm not going to tell you what to do."

"Wh-why not?" asked Jason, who, like most children, apparently expected all adults to feel free to boss him around.

"Because I'm not your father." Trey glanced quickly at Rachel.

"I wish you were."

Jason's eyes went wide as he spoke; he covered his mouth with one freckled hand. Trey was equally stunned.

The slamming of a door broke the tension and Thom T., clattered out to welcome Trey back.

NOW RACHEL PUT renewed effort into finishing up her report for Thom T. When she wasn't working at the library, she spent her spare time sorting and classifying documents.

Funny, out of all these boxes and reams of material, she hadn't yet found Trey's birth certificate. She had pieced together considerable information about the man who would be Trey's father—if Trey really was a member of the Taggart family. She even had a letter John Smith had written in 1962 to his parents, Barbara and Thomas Taggart Smith of New Orleans.

In it he'd spoken glowingly of his infant son, Tommy, and less glowingly of his wife, referring to her only as *that* woman. There was no envelope with the letter, so Rachel had no idea where it had been mailed from.

Trey stuck his head through the doorway. "You busy?"

As always, her heart leaped at the sound of his voice, but she merely gave him a cool glance. "As you see." She indicated the piles of paper. "Trey, you said your mother's name was Linda, right?"

He nodded and stepped inside. He wore Levi's and a chambray shirt, not his usual mode of dress. She didn't care what he wore or didn't wear; he looked great.

"And your father's name was Jack. Was that a nickname for John, do you suppose?"

He shrugged. "Damned if I know. Rachel—" he half lowered his lids over teasing eyes "—let's get out of here for a while."

Her heart skipped a beat. "I'm much too busy."

"With that?" He waved her excuse aside. "You're just humoring the old man and we both know it. Let's go have a beer at the Yellow Rose, maybe dance a little. Talk a little...."

"I don't go to bars." She began to rake papers toward her, messing up the neat piles. The silence stretched out until she had to notice. At last she looked up....

Into laughing eyes and a sensual mouth that said, "Don't tell *me* what you do or don't do, Lizzie."

She felt herself blush to the very roots of her hair. "I've forgotten all that," she said haughtily. "I thought you had, too."

"Why, you little...liar! Don't tell me you forgot what it was like, naked under the stars . . ."

"Please stop! Someone might hear you!" She glanced around frantically but no one—not Thom T. nor Jason nor Laddy—was in sight.

"Just the two of us, making long, slow, sweet love. Let's do it again, Lizzie." He leaned forward, his palms flat on the polished wooden dining table.

"It wasn't love, it was only sex." She was breathing hard despite her best efforts to remain calm. A cold film of perspiration covered her forehead. She wanted to scream *Yes!* and throw herself into his arms. "And it'll never happen again—not with you, anyway. Maybe someday with a man who'll understand and care for me as a woman, not just a-an available body...."

He leaned closer still, until his face was only inches from hers. He bared even white teeth, the creases in his lean cheeks deepening. "Understand what? Lizzie isn't your evil twin, babe, she's the best part of you, the spontaneous part, the part—"

He stopped short, licking his lips, and Rachel stared, remembering all the wonderful things that mouth was capable of doing to and for her.

"Lizzie's the part of me that's caused most of the trouble in my life," she said breathlessly. "I've spent years learning how to control...Lizzie...and then you came along. No, Trey, it's not worth the risk."

Trey straightened, and for a moment an expression of utter frustration crossed his face. "Suit yourself." He gave her a look so intense it nearly curled her toes. "Maybe you can forget, but I sure as hell can't."

HE'D TRIED; God knows, he'd tried, he told himself on the drive into town. Frustration had put him into a dangerous mood, heightened by her rejection. Curiously enough, his first thought had been of Dixie Baker, but she wasn't at home. "If it's important, you can call me tonight between nine and ten, or tomorrow morning before eleven," her answering machine had commanded. None of that wimpy "Please, Thank you," and "I'll get right back to you" crap from Dixie. Do it her way or screw you!

He left a message, anyway. "I decided to forgive you for being a snob, but you missed your chance. See you around."

He'd have liked the company, he admitted, leaving the pickup in the parking lot of the Yellow Rose. The saloon was moderately busy for a Thursday evening.

The bartender appeared. "What'll it be?"

"Club soda with a twist."

The bartender's eyebrows climbed but he made no comment. Maybe he was getting used to Trey's peculiar drinking habits.

Times like this, Trey wished he was on friendlier terms with alcohol. He'd like to get drunk as a skunk, pick up some good-looking but uncomplicated babe and let her have her way with him. Looking around the room, his glance locked with that of a classy blonde sitting with a couple of less spectacular women near the front windows.

She caught him looking at her, smiled and licked her lips. Her frankly approving gaze drifted down his body.

Which obediently sprang to attention. Trey swallowed hard and thought of cold showers, icy streams and blizzards. It didn't help.

Why not go for it and put Thom T.'s "gift" to good use? She looked like a tourist; they'd go to her motel and do it, and he'd feel better afterward.

Sure he would—*goddammit, if Rachel wasn't going to come through for him when he needed her*—but how about turning that around? Maybe she'd needed him, but he'd been thinking with a part of his body other than his brain.

The blonde's two companions rose and, with a flurry of overblown goodbyes and darting glances, departed. The coast was now clear. The situation could not be more obvious if a neon sign flickered above the table: Take Me, I'm Yours.

He picked up his glass and pushed away from the bar. He'd do it. He didn't like hard-to-get women. There was a limit and he'd reached it with Rachel.

The blonde smiled. He smiled back and sauntered toward her, but something caught his attention—a little silver car zipping by the window, traveling much too fast.

He knew at once it was Rachel's, and also knew that something was wrong. He didn't know how he knew, he just did. He gave the blonde his most ingratiating smile. "Excuse me," he said. "Maybe another time . . ."

Placing his glass of club soda on her table, he sprinted out of the Yellow Rose.

10

RACHEL'S CAR stood at the curb in the No Parking zone before the small town jail a block down Main Street. With a quick, guilty wave through the window to the scowling blonde, Trey set off at a quick jog.

He barged in to find Rachel facing Sheriff's Deputy Pete Snow across the scarred width of the lawman's desk. At the sudden interruption, she looked around.

"You! This is none of your business, Trey Smith."

He saw her flushed, unhappy face and tried to keep from softening. "I'm making it my business. What's Laddy done now?"

"What makes you so sure he's done anything?"

Pete made an exasperated sound. "Give it up, Rachel. Your brother's an accident lookin' for a place to happen. Everybody knows it, even this Yankee, here." Pete finished with a slightly apologetic glance.

Trey grinned. "I repeat, what'd the kid do?"

Rachel turned her back on him so Pete provided the answer.

"Got tanked and busted up the Alamo Cantina. I got him coolin' off back there." Pete gestured toward the half-open door with the barred window.

"Good place for him," Trey commented.

Rachel whirled. "No! Pete, you've got to let him out."

Pete looked resolute, if uncomfortable. "Now, Rachel, you know . . ."

"I'll pay for any damage. Just let him out, please!" She looked on the verge of tears. Cool, calm, confident Rachel Cox was about to lose it.

Pete shook his head stubbornly. "I don't wanna do that, Rachel. For the boy's own good."

"You don't know what you're talking about!" She clasped her trembling hands. "Pete, you know my father. He spent a lot of nights in that jail cell, and did it do him any good? No. All it did was humiliate him before his family and the entire town. I can't let that happen to Laddy."

"But your daddy was a goner before you were even born. There's still time to help Laddy," Pete argued. "He's young. Maybe he can still learn, if we can get his attention. Damn, woman, the way you smother the boy..."

The color drained from Rachel's face and Pete broke off. His panicky glance flew to Trey.

"Let me talk to her," Trey suggested.

"Gladly." Pete edged toward the door. "I'll go grab me a cup of coffee. Be back in a few minutes."

Trey waited until the deputy closed the door, then turned to the distraught woman. "Rachel," he said, "the guy's right."

"You don't know anything about it," she flared. "Why don't you mind your own business, for once?"

Why, indeed? Trey sighed. "In the immortal words of Thom T. Taggart, I'm a glutton for punishment. Don't know why. Every time I get involved in other people's problems I get my ass kicked."

"Then don't get involved. Just leave and go back to whatever you were doing."

Trey recalled the blonde and sighed again. "Sorry, babe, but I've missed that boat. So I might as well tell you that the deputy gave it to you straight. Laddy'll learn his lesson the hard way or not at all. Let him cool his heels overnight in a jail cell, give him time to think about his sins. Because if he doesn't see the error of his ways, the hooch will eventually get him. One way or the other, it'll get him."

She gave him a scornful glance, but he saw the fear as well. "You're such an expert, but you hardly even drink. I grew up with an alcoholic, and I can tell you from personal experience that nagging won't make him quit."

He wasn't getting through to her. *This is the showdown*, he thought; either he spilled his guts or he backed off and shut up about it, once and for all.

"Some expert," she said, dismissing him by turning her back.

Trey's scalp tightened and his gut clenched. Now was the time to let her screw up her life, her brother's and her son's without further help from him. He'd known all along that he'd eventually walk, but now the perfect moment had arrived and something wouldn't let him do it. To his surprise and consternation, he found himself grabbing her by the arms and spinning her around.

"Nagging's not what I had in mind. And as for how I know what I know, my second—no, it was my third foster mother who was the drunk. She passed out with a bottle and knocked over a heater that set the house on fire."

Her expression softened with quick sympathy. "I'm sorry, but that was an isolated incident. Just because one person . . ."

"Lady, you're wearing blinders."

She flinched and he became aware he'd tightened his grip on her arms. He forced himself to loosen his hold but didn't let her go; he was afraid that if he did, she'd bolt. And he had to make her listen.

"One of my foster brothers died in that fire. We were both ten—our birthdays were only a few weeks apart. It could just as easily have been me, Rachel. I don't know why the hell it wasn't. That's when I realized nothing in this life is certain. Timmy was—"

He broke off abruptly. He hadn't allowed himself to think about Timmy for a long time. "He was a really good kid, but that wasn't enough to keep him alive. Alcohol killed him and he didn't even drink."

"Trey . . ." She looked frightened. "Please don't—"

"My foster brother at the next place died of a drug overdose. We weren't close. He was sixteen and I was about eleven. He thought he was a real bad dude, which he probably was. But when he OD'd, his mother—my foster mother—went off the deep end. She couldn't understand why he had died but I was still alive. So I got moved again."

"Oh, Trey . . . How horrible for a little boy."

"Jason's a little boy. What if he gets hurt by Laddy's drinking?" She flinched, but Trey was merciless. He shook her, hard. "Rachel, life is full of tough choices. I didn't mean to get involved in your problems with your brother but he's going down. The only question is, who's he taking with him?"

"Laddy would never hurt Jason or me. We Coxes stick together because we're all we've got."

Trey groaned. "And you think I'm a danger to you in this two-bit hick town? Think again. Laddy's a helluva lot more likely to drag you down than I ever was."

She squeezed her eyes shut and an expression of pain crossed her face. "I have to take that chance because he's my brother and I love him," she whispered. "When you love someone, you . . . you give them the benefit of the doubt. Surely you understand that."

Trey couldn't recall anyone ever giving him the benefit of the doubt, except maybe Thom T. What would it be like to love—or be loved—that much? He couldn't even imagine, since he wasn't at all sure he even knew what love was. He was sure no one had ever loved him, nor did he expect anyone ever would.

"All I understand," he said, "is that Laddy's made his bed, but you won't let him lie in it. For *his* sake, back off."

The door opened and Pete entered. "So what'll it be?" he asked.

Both men looked at Rachel. She had regained her composure and stood before them, arms at her sides. Trey saw an uncertainty in her eyes that had never been there before, and felt an unaccustomed leap of hope that she might yet do the right thing.

"I . . . I want . . ." She licked her lips. "I want you to release my brother," she said quickly, turning to Pete. "I'll be responsible for all damage."

Hope gave way to bitter disappointment. "Don't do this," Trey said. "He'll only—"

"I have to. Please understand. All he has to do is tell me he'll try and I'll believe him." Rachel turned her appeal to Pete. "May I see him now?"

The deputy sighed. "Sure, why not?"

He gestured to the door. She passed through without another glance in Trey's direction. Pete rolled his eyes, then followed.

Trey walked to the window and stared at the dusky street. What the hell was he waiting for? She'd rejected him along with his advice, yet he stayed where he was, hopelessly entangled in the affairs of Showdown's lady librarian.

The inner door swung open and Laddy stood there, breathing fire. Bruised and battered from this latest scrape, his angry, bloodshot gaze settled on Trey with hostile intent.

"You son of a bitch!" he shouted. "You think I couldn't hear what you were sayin' out here? Where the hell do you get off, talkin' against me to my own sister?" He took a step forward, fists rising.

Trey glared at the boy who'd caused so much trouble; clearly much more was still to come. He'd had enough; his patience was at an end. He bared his teeth, but spoke softly. "I've dicked around with you long enough, kid. You want to settle this here and now, come and get it." He gestured with the fingers of his left hand.

Laddy howled and launched himself across the room. Trey stepped forward to meet his adversary, overwhelmed by the warrior spirit. Then he remembered who he was and who this boy was, and saw that Rachel had appeared in the doorway, a look of horror on her face.

So instead of beating the kid to a pulp as he longed to do, Trey sidestepped him, reached out and neatly flipped Laddy through the air in a complete circle. The boy hit the floor flat on his back and lay there, stunned.

Trey leaned over his fallen foe, sorry it had been so easy. Alcohol fumes struck him square in the face and he recoiled. "Listen to me, you sorry sack of shit," he hissed between his teeth. "Your sister's gone way out on a limb for you. If you let her down, I will personally kick your butt up between your shoulder blades. *¿Comprende?*"

Laddy rolled onto his stomach and pushed to his hands and knees. For a moment his head swung loosely back and forth. Gathering himself, he lunged upward.

"Why don't yawl get off my back?" he cried, weaving where he stood. "I'm sick and tired of everybody telling me what I can and can't do." He swung his head and glared at Rachel through bloodshot eyes. "And that includes you!"

She held out a hand in a placating gesture. "Let's go home, Laddy. Ill fix you a pot of hot coffee and we can talk. Nobody's trying to tell you what to do. We're worried, that's all."

"*He's* worried about me?" Laddy sneered at Trey. "He made a fool outa me."

"You did that all on your own, kid," Trey suggested dryly. "Several times, in fact."

"And he stole Jason away—his 'fections, I mean." Laddy's reddened eyes narrowed.

"You're mistaken." All Rachel's attention was concentrated on the angry young man. "Jason loves his uncle—"

"And you—he's gonna steal you away, too. God-damn Yankee!" Laddy looked at Trey with utter loathing. It was obvious the boy would launch another attack if he thought he had the slightest chance of prevailing. He didn't. He knew that now, to his pain and humiliation.

"What's the use? None of you understand." Turning, Laddy stumbled from the jail. Rachel started after him, but Pete caught her arm.

"There goes a boy who ain't learned a damned thing," the deputy said in disgust. "Set down and sign these papers, Rachel, and then I'm gonna go out and pick him up again. Because he's nothin' but a damned powder keg, and no matter what you say..."

Rachel looked completely played out. "I won't say another word."

Trey clamped his teeth and tried to think hard thoughts. He was *not* going to give her another chance to kick him. He was *not* going to put his arms around her and tell her not to worry, everything would be all right because he'd *make* everything all right. He was *not* going to help her chase after her trouble-making brother.

Then she turned those wounded hazel eyes upon him. "You were right," she whispered. "Oh, Trey, you were right all along."

Well, hell, what could he do after that?

SHE DROVE HOME, Trey following in the pickup truck. She was sure that was where Laddy would go, since he didn't have a car and wasn't in any shape to do much walking.

Trey hadn't waited for an invitation to accompany her and she was glad of that. He really had behaved like a gentleman throughout this entire ordeal. She was well aware that he could have done serious damage to Laddy back there without even working up a sweat. He could also have made her eat crow.

He'd done neither, and for that she was grateful. But his generosity didn't change the fact that she'd been wrong. She owed Trey Smith an abject apology.

Laddy wasn't at the house. Together, Rachel and Trey walked through every room, but he simply hadn't been there. Back in the living room, worry and concern began to grow into anger.

"Maybe he's trying to walk some of it off," Trey suggested. He sprawled on the couch, legs stretched before him. "He was still pretty wasted when he ran out of there."

She knew what those legs looked like without the denim covering. Desire hit her, so intense that it dried her mouth and moistened the palms of her hands. How had she been so stupid? This was a man in a million, whether he was a Taggart or not.

"Maybe," she agreed halfheartedly. She licked her lips. "Trey, I . . . I want to apologize to you."

His dark brows soared. "What for?"

"For being so blind where my brother's concerned, for one thing. I'm so scared for him my stomach hurts, but I'm more scared realizing that in the state he's in, he could hurt somebody else."

Trey cocked his head to one side and patted the cushion beside him. His wonderful smile appeared, slow and sexy. "Come sit down, Rachel Elizabeth," he said, "and let's talk about this."

It was both command and invitation. She stared at him, struck by the indescribable certainty that a decision now would change the course of her life.

But it was just a simple thing he wanted, to have her sit beside him. Moving woodenly, she crossed the room and joined him on the couch.

He picked up one of her hands and examined each individual finger with care. "What's the second thing?" he asked.

Her heart fluttered and her pulse drummed in her ears. She drew a shuddering breath. "S-second thing?"

"You apologized for being blind about your brother, 'for one thing.' What else are you apologizing for?"

She curled her fingers through his and held on tight. "For not trusting you."

He looked uncomfortable. "Hey, I'm no saint. I knew you were Lizzie all along and didn't let on. . . ."

"But I was the one pretending to be someone I wasn't. It was stupid and childish."

"Yes, but I wasn't entirely honest, either. And I made a fool out of Laddy."

"He deserved it."

"That's true." Trey laid her palm flat against his chest. Through the soft cotton she felt the throb of his heart. He gave her a crooked grin. "I more or less tricked you into my bed—or sleeping bag, as the case may be."

"I deserved it." She drew a breath, almost choking. "I hope I deserve it . . . again. I know I want it."

He stared at her, lips parted. "Is this the prim and proper lady librarian talking? I can't believe what I'm hearing."

"Then I'll say it in plain English." She swallowed hard. "I want you, Trey Smith. Have I so completely burned my bridges that you're not interested any longer?"

"I'm interested, all right." He looked at their entwined hands. "I haven't been interested in any other woman since I met Liz in the Alamo Cantina."

He slipped one arm around her and lifted her onto his lap. She couldn't believe she'd let him do it; she felt awkward and uncertain, but was determined not to allow her inhibitions to spoil this moment.

She slipped one arm around his neck and guided his head to rest against her breast, feeling very safe and secure with him.

She ran the fingers of one hand through his hair and tilted his head back so she could look into his face. "You really don't understand why appearances are so important to me, do you?"

"No, but I understand this." He shifted her on his lap, leaving no doubt as to his meaning or his desire.

That knowledge filled her with surprised pleasure. She wasn't used to having men want her. If any had—besides Bobby, of course—she hadn't known it.

Trey touched her cheek. "You're blushing. You're really an innocent, you know that?"

She dipped her head. "Not innocent—dumb. I've never . . . I've never been involved in anything like this before."

"Anything like what?" He nuzzled her throat and she let her head fall to one side to give him free access.

"Wh-whatever this is between us." She was almost afraid to put a name to it for fear of making a fool of herself. "A love affair, a quick roll in the hay, whatever."

He stopped kissing her and moved her around until he could see her expression. He was frowning, and she wondered what she had done wrong this time.

Gently he touched the side of her face. "I'm about to break one of my cardinal rules," he said. "I don't like to get involved in other people's business, and I especially don't like to ask or be asked personal questions. But jeez, I can't let this pass."

Cold dread slipped down her spine. "What do you want to know?" she asked in a small voice.

"How many men have you slept with?"

She had never imagined being asked such a question. "What difference does it make?" she hedged.

"None, if it's more than one," he shot back. "I'd never have pursued you the way I did if I'd thought you were practically a virgin."

"I'm not," she objected halfheartedly. "I'm a mature woman with a son."

"Oh, really? Then answer my question. How many men have you slept with? Excluding me, of course."

Up close like this, he simply overwhelmed her. When he touched her, looked into her eyes, withholding and promising at the same time, she couldn't imagine anything she wouldn't do to please him.

Except lie. She licked her lips, searching desperately for a way out of this morass.

"How many, Rachel Elizabeth? Less than six?"

"Six! What do you think I am, a—"

Too late, she saw he was laughing at her. Another wave of color heated her cheeks. "Stop, Trey. You're embarrassing me."

"Less than three?"

"I don't want to talk about this, okay?" With a sudden inspiration, she leaned forward and dropped a kiss upon his collarbone, exposed by the open collar of his shirt. With incredible daring she tickled his skin with the tip of her tongue.

"Not okay." His voice sounded hoarse and his breathing accelerated. "Tell me you've slept with more than one man."

She kissed the undercurve of his jaw. "Okay."

"Jeez, that's a relief. You had me worried there for a minute. So . . . how many?"

She stopped kissing him and sat up again. "You're not going to let this alone, are you?"

He shook his head.

"Then I may as well confess. I've slept with one and a half men. There, are you satisfied? Kiss me, Trey."

"Not so fast. One and a half men? You're going to have to explain that."

She sighed. "Jason's father was my first love. Then years later, while I was in college, I got really . . . restless, I guess you could say."

"No, babe, what I'd say is frustrated. I have more than a passing acquaintance with the word—and the condition."

"Well, I didn't. I don't . . . usually. You've kind of turned everything upside down for me." She stroked the side of his face, reveling in the fine, firm texture of his skin.

"Don't change the subject," he warned, but his voice sounded ragged. "You've accounted for one. How about that half?"

"Like I said, I was in college and I met a guy I kind of liked. And I decided, why not? Everybody else does it. But when the time came, I couldn't go through with it. He took pity on me and we really did sleep together, nothing more."

Trey frowned. "Why couldn't you go through with it, honey? What stopped you?"

"Why . . . ?" She frowned. At the time she hadn't dug too deeply, just assumed she'd chickened out because she had too much to lose. But she had more to lose now, and here she was, with a man who'd already made love to her on one occasion, hoping and praying he was about to do it again.

"Tell me what stopped you," he repeated.

"I guess I simply didn't—" She drew back before she could betray herself by saying, *I simply didn't love him enough . . . as I loved Bobby. As I love you.* Instead she said, "I guess the time wasn't right. He was gentleman enough to respect my feelings."

Trey reached for the buttons on her blouse with sure fingers. "I respect your feelings too, Rachel, but in another minute or two . . ." He slipped his hand inside her blouse, beneath her bra strap, and curved his fingers over the upper slope of her breast. "Do you want to make love now?"

"Yes, Trey—oh, yes!" She looked into his eyes when she said it, wanting him to know how much she meant it. "*Yes!*"

HE CARRIED HER into the bedroom, tossed her onto the bed, and proceeded to show her any number of things she'd never imagined doing and forever after, wouldn't be able to imagine doing without. A skilled and tender lover, Trey put her feelings and responses before his own as a matter of course.

She blossomed beneath this erotic, thrilling assault, trusting him more each passing moment. *Here is a man to cherish,* she thought at the moment of oneness. *Here is a man to love.*

And she did. Feeling the pressure build, Rachel knew in some dim recess of her mind that her physical response could not be so great without some further explanation.

Love. At her climax she cried out, clinging to him, knowing she would be his forever.

She came back to reality slowly, floating on a cloud of happiness. Beside her, atop the rumpled blue bedspread, Trey's strangled breathing slowly grew deep and even again. Turning onto his side with a groan of satisfaction, he smiled at her.

"You're really something," he murmured. "You know that?"

Suddenly shy again she shook her head. "No, but I'm glad you think so."

"A man of my sophisticated tastes doesn't think, he knows." He gave her an intimate pat and sat up. "I'm dry—literally. Can I bring you something from the kitchen?"

"Yourself," she said. "Just yourself."

Leaning toward him, she brushed her lips across his thigh, letting her tongue flick over hair-roughened skin. "That was wonderful, Trey!" she burst out. "Nothing's ever been so wonderful except the first time with you. I've gone crazy since, remembering and thinking nothing so wonderful would ever happen to me again."

"Not to worry, babe. There's plenty more where that came from."

He caught her by the shoulders and hauled her up to plant a quick, hard kiss upon her lips. Then he laid her back, stood up and sauntered out of the bedroom, his walk cocky and his pale backside enchanting.

TREY STEPPED into the kitchen and slumped back against the doorframe. His gut clenched and cold sweat covered his forehead.

What the hell had this woman done to him? He felt helpless with her, incapable of maintaining the core of indifference that always allowed him to preserve a certain emotional distance, even from women he bedded. He needed to reassert his independence and needed to do it fast.

Walking woodenly to the refrigerator, he pulled out a half-gallon carton of milk, tore open the flap and chugalugged half the contents. A man could get addicted to sex that great. A man could get addicted to the woman who provided it, so sweetly and innocently that he felt as if he were taking a virgin. A man could start thinking about a future with such a woman. . . .

A man could fall in love.

He slammed the refrigerator door and stood there, quivering from head to foot. He wasn't even sure what loving felt like; he'd never been in love and had never expected to be. Love wasn't an emotion to be trusted, and he'd long since written off the possibility of finding it.

As she had apparently written off sex. Talk about a waste. And yet, he couldn't help the swell of pride he felt at the knowledge that he and he alone had breached her defenses—since Bobby Baker, anyway.

He was considerably less willing to acknowledge she was very close to breaching his defenses in return.

Carrying the milk carton, he started back toward the bedroom. He'd make it clear that he would still be leaving as soon as she'd convinced Thom T. that Trey was not a long lost Taggart. Until then, they could certainly enjoy an adult relationship based on mutual—

The front door flew open with a bang and Trey stopped short, suddenly conscious that he was wearing nothing but a day-old beard and a stupid expression. There in the doorway stood Dixie Baker, hair and eyes equally wild.

But not made that way by finding herself confronted by a naked man, Trey decided. Her glance flicked over him as if she walked in on such sights every day of the week and twice on Sunday.

She took an awkward step forward. "Trey, is Rachel here?"

He tipped his head toward the bedroom. "In there. Dixie, what is it?"

She spoke precisely, but her voice was under enormous pressure. "It's Laddy. There's been an accident. He was driving down Dead Man's Curve with Jason and—"

"No!" Rachel appeared in the bedroom doorway, hair in disarray and the robe over her shoulders hanging unevenly. She looked very much like a woman who'd just made love—and who now was about to pass out.

11

RACHEL SCREAMED her son's name and threw herself forward in blind panic. Trey caught hold of her to keep her from running right over Dixie in her fear and confusion.

"Jason's all right," Dixie said hastily, retreating a step. "He's outside in my car—"

"I don't believe you!" Rachel struggled against Trey's grasp. "If he's all right, why didn't he come in?"

"Because I was afraid you'd react just as you have. The boy doesn't need to see his mother in such a state." Dixie kept her glance pinned to Rachel, apparently determined to ignore the implications of the scene before her.

Trey felt all the starch run out of the woman in his arms as she acknowledged the truth of Dixie's words. She slumped against him, trembling.

"I'm sorry." She almost choked on the words. "I'm all right now. Please, Mrs. Baker, tell me what happened."

"Of course, dear. Uhh..." Dixie glanced pointedly at Trey's naked haunches. "I'd been to my quilting circle out at Ruby Turner's and was on my way home. Thom T.'s big Cadillac was in front of me, weaving all over the road, and when it turned toward Dead Man's Curve, I followed on an impulse."

She paused significantly. "Thank heaven I did, because the car didn't make that last curve."

"Laddy was driving?" Rachel asked faintly.

"Yes, and Jason was with him—buckled into his seat belt, or I'm sure he'd have been seriously hurt. Your brother was thrown from the car. There was . . ."

Dixie faltered for the first time, and Trey was suddenly aware of how harrowing it must have been for her to arrive first at such a scene.

"There was a lot of blood, but the ambulance got there fast. I took Jason with me to spare him that." Suddenly she smiled. "He's such a good boy, Rachel. You've done a fine job with him."

Rachel drew herself up stiffly. "Thank you. Did Jason see a doctor?"

Dixie nodded. "Dr. Preston says he'll be stiff and sore tomorrow, and he'll have assorted bumps and bruises. Other than that, he'll be fine. Laddy . . . well, at least they're hopeful. If you'd seen the car shoot off that curve you'd be grateful he's even alive."

Rachel took a step away from Trey. "I have to see Jason." She stopped short. "No, I have to go to the hospital—oh!" She looked helplessly at Trey, as if seeking guidance.

Dixie was looking at him, too—all of him this time, an *Oh, my!* expression on her face as if she'd just realized he was buck naked. Rachel frowned, then followed the other woman's gaze and blanched. Trey's grin felt slightly off center but under the circumstances, he was proud of himself for smiling at all.

Rachel stepped in front of him and threw her arms wide. "This isn't how it looks," she exclaimed breathlessly.

Dixie's already arched brows soared. "My dear, this is *exactly* how it looks," she said calmly. "I didn't just fall off a turnip truck. It couldn't possibly be anything else."

"But I can expl—"

"Don't bother." Dixie might just as well have said, *Don't waste your breath.* "You're needed at the hospital, so why don't I take Jason home with me?"

"But . . . but . . ." Rachel glanced around desperately. "He doesn't know you."

"Of course he does. We've spoken on any number of occasions."

"But he'll be scared—he'll be worried about his uncle."

"He'll be more scared and worried if he sees his mother near hysterics," Dixie pointed out tartly.

"But . . ."

Trey knew what she didn't say: *But I'm afraid to send him off with you because you're his grandmother and neither one of you knows it!* Taking pity on her, he intervened. "That's the best solution, honey." The endearment fell easily from his lips. "You'll want to get on over to the hospital and that's no place for the boy."

He met Dixie's glance and found it hopeful, yet guarded. This meant more to her than she cared to reveal. "Thanks, Dixie," he said. "It's the best solution. We'll call before we come for the boy."

"Don't hurry." Dixie's face glowed with a pleasure she couldn't conceal, even on this grim occasion. "He can stay the night, if you like. My son's room—well, I can put Jason up with no problem."

At the mention of Dixie's son, Rachel's shoulders sagged, but she gave no other sign of distress. "Thank you, then," she said. "Tell Jason I love him and I'll speak to him soon."

"I will. And I'll pray for your brother." Dixie half turned. "Rachel, before I go . . . I want to apologize for what I said the other day."

Rachel frowned. "Wh-what you said?"

"About the apple never falling far from the tree. I said it without thinking, which is certainly no excuse. Trey told me you'd overheard." Dixie smiled wryly. "Just before he called me a snob."

"He called you that?" Rachel gave him an uncomprehending glance.

"I'm not conceding he's right, you understand, but I'm . . . considering his point of view." Dixie looked as if she might say something more, turned instead and let herself out, closing the door gently behind her. Once she was gone, Rachel swung toward Trey.

He read the panic on her face. "It'll be okay," he promised, not sure he was telling her the truth. "Let's throw on some clothes and get over to the hospital."

They were halfway there before the familiar terror began to creep up on him.

RACHEL SLUMPED against the door to Laddy's hospital room, emotionally drained. Her brother was still unconscious following surgery and no one knew if he would live or die.

But she couldn't fall apart now. Quickly she looked around for her source of strength, her anchor, and found him on the far side of the waiting room. Trey hovered near the outside door, grim-faced. That was where he'd stationed himself upon arrival, declining to budge. He'd even refused to enter Laddy's room.

She shouldn't have been surprised, Rachel thought tiredly. There certainly was no love lost between her brother and this man who meant so much to her. Slowly she walked to him.

He refused to meet her gaze. "How's he doing?"

"I'm . . . not sure. Dr. Preston expressed guarded optimism, but Laddy looks awful, hooked up to all those tubes. They're giving him blood and—"

Trey fumbled for a chair and sat down abruptly. He looked a little green. "I don't need the gory details," he muttered.

"Fine! I won't bore you with them, then." Hurt by his apparent lack of interest, she glanced around for a pay phone. "I should call Jason."

"And tell him what? You don't know anything yet."

"I know I'm not happy having him at Mrs. Baker's." That sounded so snappish that she was instantly contrite. Before she could apologize, Trey gave a nasty laugh.

"You should be grateful the kid has someplace to go until this is over. Dixie'll take good care of him."

"And us, too, no doubt."

"What's that supposed to mean?" Trey gritted his teeth and glared at her.

"Just that Dixie Baker is the worst gossip in town." Why did he have to choose *now* to get temperamental? "I'm sure she's already spreading the good news—once a Cox, always a Cox. Blood will tell."

His eyes glinted dangerously. "What the hell are you talking about?"

"About Mrs. Baker finding us together that way, you naked and me just as good as."

"So?" His angry scowl challenged her. "Were you ashamed of me?"

"Of you? No! Ashamed of myself, mostly." She sat down beside him and buried her head in her hands for a moment, feeling the crushing weight of worry and disappointment. Suddenly she looked up, painfully aware that this disapproving stranger was not the tender lover in whose arms she had found such bliss.

All her fear and worry boiled to the surface. "You've ruined my reputation all over again," she accused, "and this time I'll never get it back. I hope you're happy!"

She jumped to her feet and stared at him fiercely, even though some last shred of conscience warned her she was being unfair.

"I'm sure as hell not happy!" he roared, closer to losing control than she had ever seen him. "Dixie Baker is a decent woman—not perfect, maybe, but at least she had the guts to apologize to you. She won't say a word about finding us in a *compromising situation!*"

He shouted the last two words at a nurse hurrying past; she darted them a startled glance and continued on her way. "But if she does," he continued relentlessly, "so what? I, for one, don't care if the whole world—"

He stopped short, his jaw dropping.

"If the whole world, what?" Rachel cried. "Knows I slept with Thom T. Taggart's damn Yankee visitor? It won't hurt your reputation any, but then, what could?"

HE DIDN'T CARE if the whole world knew he lov—

Goddamn it, no! He *cared* for Rachel Cox, that much he'd admit. He wasn't even going to *think* the "L" word in the same sentence.

In the first place, it would be unrequited. She valued too many people before him—her son, her brother— and too many things. Like her reputation.

Her damned reputation. She hadn't so much as touched him since they'd walked into this accursed hospital, or let him touch her.

But because he cared for her, he'd stick his neck out one more time like the damn fool he was. And she was going to step on it, but what the hell?

"If you spent half the time and effort on living as you do worrying about what people think, you'd be a hell of a lot happier!" he yelled at her.

"Look who's giving advice. A guy whose idea of happiness is rolling cars and falling down stairs— alone!"

Trey groaned. He didn't need to be standing here in a damned hospital, fighting with a woman whose only interest in him was below the waist! Why tiptoe? Just let him say what he needed to say and get it over with, he raged at himself.

Grabbing her by the shoulders, he glared at her. "If Laddy pulls through, let him live his own life. *And let Dixie Baker get to know her grandson.*"

Once again the color drained from Rachel's face. "D-Dixie Baker... What are you talking about? Don't say such things!"

Her knees buckled and he guided her, none too gently, into a vinyl-covered chair. She looked to be on the verge of hyperventilating, but he wasn't about to back off.

He looked down at her bowed head. "Bobby Baker is Jason's father," he said in a voice perilously close to cracking.

He expected her to deny it peremptorily, but after a long, agonized silence, she whispered, "How did you find out?"

"I didn't find out, I guessed. Sometimes it's easier for an outsider to put two and two together." An outsider. He felt a shaft of pain; he was an outsider everywhere he went. That was all he'd ever been or ever would be.

She looked up, beseeching him with her eyes to understand. "You won't tell anyone? Promise me you won't tell."

The knife in his gut twisted. "I should. Somebody should. *You* should, Rachel."

"No. You don't understand." She shook her head violently. "It would just mean a heavier cross for Jason to bear."

"You're wrong. Nothing's worse for a boy than not knowing." That was true. He hadn't known anything about his father and it had haunted his boyhood, haunted him still. He had missed so much, growing up without the emotional support of a family. How much it would have meant to discover he had a grandmother or a father—someone to love him.

Like a great-uncle . . . like Thom T. Taggart. Finally Trey had to admit it, at least to himself; he hoped Taggart blood flowed in his veins.

"You're talking about yourself now, not Jason." Rachel's voice trembled.

"Yeah, maybe. Probably." Trey felt numb inside, the same numbness he'd been running from all his life. The only difference was, this time he couldn't run; he was not the only one at risk. "Laddy and Jason—"

The matronly nurse who'd passed by earlier came out of Laddy's room, clipboard in hand. She approached them, smiling. "How you holdin' up, hon?" She gave Rachel a comforting pat on the shoulder.

"Okay. . . I guess. Has anything happened, Jenny?"

"Mercy, no. I just wanted to tell you the doctor will be out to speak to you in a couple of minutes. He wants you to be sure to wait for him."

"I'm not going anywhere," Rachel said in a tight little voice.

"That's good." Giving her a comforting smile, Jenny left.

Rachel picked up the conversation. "Laddy and Jason, you were saying?"

Trey grimaced. "I took to both of them, Rachel. Your brother's a little ass, and your son's close to being a sissy, but I took to both of them. You know why?"

She shook her head. "I haven't the foggiest."

He let out his breath in an explosive sigh. "Because they remind me of me. Laddy's got my wild streak carried to extremes, while Jason's the other side of the coin—barely tough enough to survive. They'd both benefit from an occasional good hard kick in the butt."

Tears shimmered in her eyes. "But I've tried so hard. Why isn't love enough?"

He felt his facial muscles tighten and knew that wasn't a question he wanted to tackle. "I don't know. Maybe sometimes it is." *It would be for me.* "All I know is what I've learned the hard way. Love never came up, so I can't speak to that."

"That's a terribly sad thing to say, Trey. Don't you know anything at all about your own family?"

"A little," he said. "Not much." Weird. She'd spent all these weeks delving into the Taggart family archives, and only now had she asked Trey a direct question about his family. He supposed that until now, she hadn't been prepared to believe anything he might tell her, so why bother to ask?

He pulled his wallet from his hip pocket and flipped it open. Pawing through the cards, receipts and bills, he extracted a small, dog-eared photograph. For a moment he stared into the faces of the man and woman pictured there.

His parents. This was all he had of them. It had been taken on their wedding day and both were smiling in black-and-white glory. The man wore a navy uniform with the stripes of a first-class petty officer; the woman wore a dress of some dark color with a flower pattern, a heavy cameo pinned to her high white collar. She held a small, droopy bouquet.

Trey couldn't remember ever seeing his mother smile that happily and didn't remember his father at all. But he did recall hiding the photograph beneath his pillow at night when he was a kid.

That had been after his mother died and the endless succession of foster homes began. He'd dreamed that his father would come and take him away, but it had never happened.

Eventually someone: a social worker, a foster parent—he'd blocked out the "who"—had taken pity on him and told him his father was dead. He'd understood what he'd heard; he just hadn't believed it, and so the dream had continued unchanged.

Somewhere there had to be someone who loved him, if only that someone could find him. Even when he'd grown old enough to be on his own, it had never occurred to him that he might set out to find that someone himself. In fact, the thought had not occurred to him until this very moment.

He didn't want Jason dreaming the same hopeless dreams. The boy's father wasn't out there, but his grandmother was. And she had more than enough love to give him.

He looked up, to find Rachel watching him with a strange, yearning expression on her face. "I want to tell you something," he heard himself saying, "something I've never told anyone before." He drew a shuddering breath. "If you want to hear . . ."

"I want to hear," she whispered.

"It's about why I have this hang-up about drugs and needles and hospitals."

She looked distressed. "You don't have to, if it bothers you so much."

"Dammit, there you go again!" His anger was out of proportion, but he was too near the edge to control it. "Do you always have to try to make it easier for the other guy? Sometimes the easy way out isn't the best way."

"I'm sorry. I just thought if you don't want to talk about it . . ."

"Hell, no! I don't want to talk about it. But if I'd talked about it years ago, maybe I could have put it behind me. Which I haven't been able to do, obviously."

"Then tell me." She sat down and patted the chair beside her. "Tell me, and if I can help I will."

So he told her. He clutched the photo of the parents who had betrayed him and told Rachel what it had been like to see his mother, to see his friends and foster siblings, fall before drugs like wheat fell at harvesttime.

He told her about the hair-raising nights spent in hospital emergency rooms, far different from this quiet and supportive place. Those other rooms had been inhabited by crazed druggies and drunks, by harried doctors and nurses and by survivors racked with grief and pain.

"After a while I quit caring," he said. "It was easier."

She shook her head. "I don't believe you. If you didn't care, it wouldn't bother you so much to talk about it after all this time."

He shrugged, refusing to look at her. "It doesn't matter. All that mattered was not letting the bastards get me."

He was sweating and his heart pounded. "My best friend died. I found him with the needle . . . still sticking out of the vein." he closed his eyes for a moment. "Then they came for me."

"They came—?" She looked at him, uncomprehending.

"I knew where he'd got the stuff that killed him. The . . . people involved didn't want me talking. So they jumped me one day and dragged me into an alley and—" He shuddered, unable to go on.

He saw the horror in her eyes and wondered if it mirrored his own. "My God, they gave you drugs?" she whispered.

Trey nodded, his mouth so dry he could hardly tell her any more. "I ended up in the same hospital emergency room where I'd waited for others to die, only this time it was me. My girl came. . . ."

With her father, who hadn't believed a word of Trey's explanation. She'd been a nice girl; too bad. He'd vowed not to make that mistake again.

Rachel sat very still. "So you had no one."

He had passed through the terrors of remembrance and come out on the other side and found it possible once again to inject bravado into his tone. "Hey, that's life in the big city. Once I got out of the hospital, I swore nobody would ever get close to me with a needle again. I developed a phobia about it, I guess. I can't stand the things or anybody pointing one at me."

He shrugged as if it no longer mattered, although of course, it did. "That's my hang-up, but your brother's is worse. He abuses alcohol, and it abuses him right back."

"Yes, maybe, but you don't understand." She stirred restlessly in her chair. "Our father was there, all right, at least physically, but when he was drinking—which was most of the time—he was terribly abusive to Laddy. Is it better to have a bad father or no father at all?"

"I don't know. I wish I did." He wished he knew a lot of things, like why he'd spilled all his secrets to her. Maybe sharing those dark memories would bring him relief later, but now all he felt was exhaustion.

For a moment they sat in silence. Then Rachel's hand brushed his and Trey started. "May I?" she asked.

He looked down uncomprehendingly while she gently pried the photo from his death grip. She looked at it for a long time. "He's very handsome," she observed finally. "You look a lot like him."

He shrugged indifferently. "Do I?"

She nodded. "And your mother's very pretty." She frowned. "That cameo she's wearing—"

"Ah, there you are."

Dr. Preston approached, looking rumpled and laid-back, as usual. Instinctively Trey rose and edged away from the doctor, belatedly remembering that he was still in a hospital.

Rachel trembled, bending the photo she still held in her hands. "Doctor, is he—?"

"Calm down, Rachel. We don't need another patient." Dr. Preston grinned at Trey and extended his hand. "Glad she's got someone here with her."

"Why? The kid losing ground?"

The doctor grimaced. "A couple of pessimists, eh? As a matter of fact, I'm beginning to see some improvement. We've been giving him blood . . ."

Trey's stomach churned and he turned away slightly.

"But we're running low on our local supply."

Rachel frowned. "Can't you get more? If he needs a transfusion, I can—" She thrust out her arm, the blue veins at the inner bend of her elbow clearly visible beneath the thin skin.

The muscles in Trey's stomach clenched and he thought for a moment he was going to be sick. Clamping his teeth, he stared at the doctor's ear and tried to think of sunshine and fresh air.

Dr. Preston shook his head. "Wrong blood type, honey—just for openers. Laddy's got AB-negative, which is harder to find, so there may be some difficulty. . . ."

My blood type, Trey realized. The bottom fell out of his gut again and he saw himself lying on a table next to Laddy, connected to the boy by tubes and needles, while his life's blood drained away. . . .

"*Are you all right?*"

The doctor had a tight grip on Trey's arm, shaking it to snap him out of the near trance into which he seemed to have fallen. Trey tore his arm free and backed away.

"Nah, I'm not all right," he mumbled. He glanced wildly from the doctor to Rachel.

She put out her hand. "Trey, please...."

She'd still plead for her brother's life, even knowing Trey's terror. "So what do you want from me now, lady?" He choked back the bile rising in his throat. "Blood?"

He couldn't stand any more; he bolted.

Thom T., on his way in, nearly got mowed down at the door. "What's eatin' the boy?" he demanded, frowning at Rachel and the doctor.

She threw herself into the old man's arms. He patted her quaking shoulders as he addressed Dr. Preston. "Don't tell me that Laddy boy's done gone and—?"

"Far from it." The doctor's frown was puzzled. "In fact, I think he's going to be fine if I can just get the blood bank to rustle up some more a' his brand of tomato juice."

"That's a relief." Thom T. sighed with audible satisfaction. "Then what's got you all lathered up, gal?" He stood Rachel away from him and glared at her.

"It's Trey," she moaned.

"Now what's that boy gone and done?"

"Nothing, Thom T. It's just that—" She swallowed hard and brushed at her damp cheeks. "I'm so relieved. I know who he is now, for sure."

"Don't be too hasty." The old man fell back a step, clearly alarmed. "We cain't be sure. The boy could still turn out to be—"

"Thom T., shh." She touched her lips lightly with her fingertip. The dear old man obviously thought her news would be bad. "We don't need any more time because . . . because I'm sure."

He looked resigned. "Give it to me straight, then," he commanded, throwing back his shoulders as if anticipating a blow.

Rachel smiled through her tears. "Trey Smith *is* the long-lost Taggart you've been looking for. He's exactly who you said he was all along!"

12

RACHEL SAT beside Laddy's bed, stroking his hand while the lifesaving blood dripped into his veins. He hadn't come out of the anesthetic yet, but Dr. Preston had predicted he would very soon. She wanted to be there for him when he opened his eyes.

He looked awful. Head bandaged and dark bruises shadowing his cheekbones, he had tubes in his nose as well as his arms. He'd also fractured his left leg and lost his spleen, but for all that, he'd been incredibly lucky.

Thom T. leaned past her to look at the patient, the expression on his lined face grim. "If he hadn't been drunk, it'd probably have killed him," he announced, adding, "A' course, if he hadn't been drunk he wouldn't a' had the accident."

Rachel nodded. There was no way she could continue to defend her brother's actions after this.

"So what's Doc Preston got to say?" Thom T. demanded.

"That Laddy's going to be all right, thank God."

The old man pulled up a chair and sat down on the opposite side of the bed. "Rachel, I'm so danged sorry I let your brother take Jason with him. Virge dropped Laddy off at the house and he sent Jason in to ask. Like a danged fool, I—"

"It's not your fault or Jason's, it's Laddy's." She was so exhausted she could barely manage a comforting smile for him. "You didn't know what was going on. If there's any blame left over, it's mine. Trey warned me that something like this was bound to happen, but I wouldn't listen. I made excuses, bailed him out every time he got in trouble...."

"Trey knows about all this, huh?"

"Yes. We were together when Mrs. Baker came to tell me about the accident." She spoke calmly, still proud of herself on some level for managing somehow to hold herself together. After Trey had left, numbness had settled around her, offering a slight protection. "Thom T., about Trey... He really is a Taggart. You were right all along."

"Yep."

"No, I mean really. I know you went with your gut feeling about this, but now there's proof. He showed me a picture of his parents, and his mother was wearing that cameo brooch that belonged to Rose. I've seen it many times in old family pictures."

Tom T. grunted. "You don't say! That's good detective work, honey."

His response somehow rang false. She frowned. "I thought you'd be relieved," she said hesitantly.

"I am," he declared, too heartily.

"Then—" What was going on here? This wasn't at all the reaction she'd expected. "Okay, Thom T., you're not telling me everything. Let's have it."

He couldn't meet her gaze. "I'm afraid there's nothin' special about that cameo. I know at least three women right here in town's got near-identical pieces."

"But..." She'd been so sure the mystery was solved. "I've never seen anyone wearing them."

"They're old-fashioned, is why. I'm all shook up, or I could a' made you think... Well, never mind that. The boy's my kith and kin. I feel it in my bones and I don't need any more proof than that. Neither do you, little lady, seein' yawl's as taken with him as I am."

Long years of denial brought glib words to her lips. "What makes you think I'm—?"

The old man waved her protests aside. "Rachel, honey, I been watchin' you two moonin' over each other pert-near from day one. I'd a' thought after tonight, you both seein' how iffy life is..." He glanced significantly at Laddy. "...that you 'n' Trey would quit waltzin' around your feelin's and admit you're just plain gone on each other."

"He's not gone on me. He's gone, period." Rachel felt the first crack in the wall she'd erected around her emotions. "I can't tell you how many times he warned me about Laddy's drinking and—and other things, but I was too cowardly to listen. Now it's too late."

"It's never too late," Thom T. said staunchly. "Where there's life, there's hope. Nobody ever told you that, girl?"

"N-no, but I want to believe it." She gave Thom T. what she knew was a trembly smile. "I don't know what I can possibly do to make this right. I've doubted his motives, taken sides against him, even lied to him. And you know what? I love him. I didn't want to, but I do."

"You ever tell him that?"

"Of course not. He's a loner. He likes it that way."

Thom T.'s smile was gentle. "He may have been a loner up to now, but no man likes it that way. The boy's been hurt, too. Mebbe you ain't the only one leery about puttin' your neck out."

Hope springs eternal. "Do you think so? But how could I prove to him that I understand what he's been trying to tell me about Laddy—?"

Laddy's weak voice startled them both. "Don't tell 'im, show 'im. You can start by—" He had to pause to clear his throat before going on; his voice came out little more than a croak. "By boxin' my ears if you ever see me reach for another drink."

"Laddy." Hot tears of relief rolled down Rachel's cheeks and she squeezed his hand.

But he wasn't finished. "You can also tell that damn Yankee that . . . I'm sorry for everything." He looked at her with a world of pain and shame in his eyes, and when he added, "I am so *damned* sorry," she knew the apology was also for her.

TREY YANKED a drawer from the dresser and upended it over the suitcase lying open on his bed. There was no longer any reason to stay. Once he'd packed, he was out of here.

This time he'd screwed up major big time, letting Rachel see what a coward he was by running out of the hospital. Shame burned a hole in his gut and there wasn't a thing he could do to ease his humiliation.

Except get the hell out.

About to toss a handful of socks into the suitcase, he stopped short, remembering how she'd turned to him with those wide, beautiful eyes filled with need.

"Smith," he said out loud, "you are an unmitigated ass."

He should have supported her, not added to her problems. He should have welcomed a chance to give blood for her brother—he should be willing to face *anything* for the woman he loved.

Every hair on Trey's scalp seemed to stand on end and he forgot to breathe. Love? Damned straight: he loved Rachel Cox. And he loved old Thom T., without benefit of blood ties. And Jason, the little boy who so desperately wanted and needed a father. Hell, he even halfway liked Laddy.

Was there anything he could salvage from this mess? Any way he could convince her that he cared for her as more than a warm body and great sex? Words wouldn't do it; it was time for show, not tell.

The familiar cold sweat broke out on his forehead, the familiar weakness hit him in the gut, doubling him over and onto the bed. Every instinct for self-preservation clamored at him to grab the suitcase and scramble back to California and the life he'd led before he ever heard of a Taggart or a certain lady librarian.

Because if he stayed . . . if he tried to win her . . . he would have to face his worst nightmare.

TREY SAW HER the moment he stepped into the hospital waiting room. She was just leaving Laddy's room, her head bowed.

Everything paled before his need to comfort her, and he started forward. Catching himself, he glanced around to see if they were being observed—for her sake. That sort of thing mattered to her, and he would try to respect her feelings. A couple of women in white uniforms chatted at the nurses' station to his right. They noticed him looking at them and gave him inquiring glances.

He shook his head and walked on. She still hadn't seen him and he said her name uncertainly. She glanced up and when she saw him, her eyes went wide and her mouth formed a soft *O!* Instantly she started forward.

Trey glanced pointedly toward the nurses, now watching boldly, but Rachel didn't seem to care. She ran straight into his arms.

She kissed him as if she meant it, and he kissed her back, drawing strength from her sweetness. "I love you," she whispered against his mouth. "Oh, Trey, I've been such a coward!"

Trey felt as if he held heaven in his arms. But if he was going to keep it, deserve it, he must match her honesty. "I . . ." He swallowed hard and squeezed his eyes shut, trying to screw up his courage. He took a gulp of air and added quickly, "I love you, too."

She stiffened and he heard her voice, muffled against his throat, drift up to him. "You don't have to say that. I didn't mean to embarrass you. It's just that you've taught me so much about facing facts. I've been afraid for so long—afraid I'd slip up and disgrace myself, afraid of public opinion, afraid of Laddy's drinking, afraid I wasn't giving Jason what he needed. . . .

She leaned back in his arms and looked into his face. "Afraid that when you left, I'd never get over it. But Trey, I'm not going to be afraid anymore. I know I'm taking a chance, but you gave me the courage to do it."

He groaned. "Rachel, baby, don't give me credit I don't deserve."

"Impossible!"

She kissed his throat, then tugged him toward the chairs lined up against the wall. He wondered if she felt as weak-kneed as he did. She sank onto one with a sigh, and he smiled, realizing that she must.

She pulled him down beside her. "I want to tell you why I've kept the secret about Bobby Baker." She licked her lips and leaned her forehead against his shoulder, as if she simply couldn't get close enough to him. "I was four months pregnant when he died, but nobody knew. The army shipped his body home for burial and the whole town turned out, so I was able to be at the funeral without anyone thinking anything about it.

"At the graveside I waited until the crowd thinned out, and then tried to get a word with his mother. It scared me just to look at her, all dressed in black and so imposing. She was like a block of ice."

Rachel shivered and he held her closer. He didn't want to hear this. Whatever had happened, it was going to infringe upon his rigid code of privacy. But he could see she needed to share it. With a sudden and unexpected flash of insight, he knew he wanted her to share everything with him from now on, grief as well as joy.

He swallowed hard. "What happened?"

"I waited my turn. She looked at me as if she had no idea who I was. Well, why should she? She didn't know I'd slept with her son or that I was carrying the only grandchild she'd ever have. I wanted so desperately to tell her—I thought perhaps it would comfort her in some way. I put out my hand as I'd seen everybody else do, and she just looked at it.

"I stammered something about knowing how she felt, which was entirely the wrong thing to say. She looked me up and down as if I'd crawled out from under some rock. 'How would *you* know how I feel?'

That's exactly what she said. I remember it as clearly as if it happened yesterday. And then she said, '*My* son didn't even *know* any girls like you, Rachel Elizabeth Cox! So how can you possibly comprehend anything at all about how *I* feel?'"

"Bitch!" And he'd defended the old biddy. He'd not make that mistake again.

She shook her head. "No, you're wrong. That's what I thought—for years, actually. But now that Jason's older..." She shuddered. "If I lost my son and some little nobody tried to tell me she knew how I felt, I—I don't know what I'd do."

"Not that," he said fiercely. "No wonder you never told her."

Rachel hung her head. "To her credit, she apologized later—about two years later. Or as close as I think she can get to an apology. But it was much too late. She scared me to death when I was sixteen and she still does. Dixie Baker's a powerful force in this town."

"Then don't tell her about Jason," Trey advised flatly. "She hurt you. She doesn't deserve to know she has a grandson. If she were a man I'd—"

"Shh." Rachel stroked his lips with her fingertips, her smile as soft as her touch. "I want to. You see, I've been terrified all these years that someone would find out or even guess the truth. I'm still afraid, but..."

She looked at him, and despite the way her body trembled in his arms, he saw her eyes were clear and untroubled. "You were right. Both Jason and Dixie should know. Will you come with me when I tell them... please?"

"Hell, yes!" Of course he would. Anywhere. He'd go anywhere with her, do whatever it took to be worthy of the love and admiration he saw shining through her understandable apprehension.

"But first," he surprised himself by adding, "I'm going to give blood for Laddy." He cupped her face and dropped a light kiss upon her lips, which only left him wanting more. "If you can face up to your worst nightmare, I sure as hell can do the same." A shudder shook him and he hung on to her tightly until it passed.

She knew what a hurdle this was for him; he saw it in her expression. Despite his fear and loathing, he also felt a kind of exhilaration that was completely new to him.

"You'd do that for me?" she whispered.

"Yes—if you don't give me time to think about it," he responded with brutal honesty.

"Thank you," she breathed. "Thank you. You're wonderful, but it's not necessary. You misunderstood what the doctor said earlier. Laddy's got all the blood he needs."

Trey's stomach muscles clenched. "Then he's going to be all right?"

"Yes, darling. And you were right about Laddy, too. From now on I'm going to let him stand on his own two feet. I love my brother and I hope I'll always be there for him but he's a man, not a boy. I'm even going to start by calling him by his proper name—Lee."

Blessed relief washed over Trey; he felt dizzy with it. *I'm off the hook!* he thought exultantly. *I don't have to do the one thing that turns me into a sniveling coward.*

But no. Almost immediately he realized there was a principle involved here. He had to conquer his unreasoning fear of needles, just as Rachel had to master her fear of public censure.

His blood could go into the public supply and perhaps save a life, to make up for the blood that had already saved the life of his future brother-in-law. Because
he was going to marry Rachel Cox; if she'd have him,
he was going to marry her and spend the rest of his life
loving her.

Through lips so stiff that he could hardly force out
the words, Trey rasped, "Let me do this before I change
my mind."

"God, I love you!" She hugged him tight. "Want me
to come with you?"

He looked at her, seeing her eyes shining with sympathy and love. He felt faint with dread—he who had
jumped off tall buildings and out of airplanes, had
plummeted to the ocean's depths, ridden wild horses
down sheer canyon walls and driven automobiles
where angels feared to fly.

He wanted her beside him more than anything in the
world, now and forever more, so of course he said,
"Hell, no!"

She laughed, a sound of delight that produced a
sheepish smile from him. "I knew you'd say that," she
murmured, "but I'm not ready to let you out of my sight
yet. Humor me, will you, darling?"

He knew what she was doing; it was plain as the knot
in his stomach. But that didn't stop him from being
grateful. "Have I mentioned that I love you?" he demanded. "Damn, but we'll be good together!"

Extending one arm, he flexed his biceps. "Bring on
Dr. Frankenstein—but make it quick before I change
my mind!"

RACHEL PLUCKED Trey's sandals from the To Pack pile. "Surely you don't want to take these?"

"To Russia in January? Hell, yes!" But he was laughing when he said it, and when he swept her into his arms for a kiss.

The month since he'd married this woman had been the happiest of Trey's life. Sometimes he lay awake at night long after she'd drifted off to sleep, trying to convince himself that this was really happening.

And to him—Trey Smith, unloved and unwanted as far back as he could remember. Now he had not only a wife he adored but a whole new family, complete with son and brother-in-law. He'd have liked being related to Thom T. as well but wouldn't quibble about that. He already had more than he'd ever dreamed existed.

He deepened the kiss. As always, he felt her desire surge to match his own. The passionate nature he'd sensed in her had flourished, bringing them both infinite joy. Maybe if they hurried, they'd have time for a quick—

"Ahem." Thom T. leaned through the doorway, clearing his throat. "Dixie just drove up with the boy."

Trey groaned and released Rachel, whose flushed cheeks and glowing eyes gave her feelings away. The difference now was, she didn't care who saw or knew.

She patted his cheek. "Later," she whispered.

God, he was proud of her. He watched her greet their son, who'd spent this last weekend in Texas with his grandmother. Dixie gave Rachel a quick hug and a kiss on the cheek.

"I'll come visit yawl in Russia," she promised. Trey, for one, believed her. "I can't say I'm glad you're goin' but I understand . . . I guess."

She crossed the room to hug Trey as well. He supposed he'd begun to take the place of her dead son—in many ways. At first that possibility had made him downright queasy, but he was getting used to it.

Hell, he'd always liked Dixie. She'd made mistakes, but who hadn't? If Rachel could forgive her, he sure as hell could.

Now that he knew Dixie better, he understood why everybody in town feared her displeasure. Everybody but Jason, who had discovered he could do no wrong where his grandmother was concerned. Without trying, the boy had mellowed her, giving her something more important to think about than everybody else's business.

The boy gave her one last embrace. "Thanks, Grandma," he said, kissing her cheek. "I had a good time." Across her shoulder his glance met Trey's.

"You want to go finish packing, sport?"

"Sure, Pop."

Pop. Every time Jason said it, Trey felt a jolt of pleasure. And one of these days, when the time was right—when he and Rachel could bear to share each other—another little person would call him Pop.

Awesome.

Dixie left with a final flurry of farewells, passing Lee on his way in.

"I'm pullin' out for Austin and just wanted to say goodbye," he announced. "Classes start Monday, so I won't be seein' you again before you leave."

Rachel threw her arms around her brother. "I'm proud of you," she said.

Trey saw tears in her eyes and turned away. They were so attuned to each other now that they seemed to feel each other's emotions, but if there was one thing he didn't want to do, it was get all misty-eyed over his brother-in-law. So the kid was starting college and hadn't had a drink since he got out of the hospital—he was still no damned saint.

Lee offered his hand to Trey and they shook. "Take care of her," the boy said, his tone gruff. "Why the hell she wants to follow you clear around the world beats me, but I haven't been able to talk her out of it."

Trey knew Lee hadn't tried. "Watch your smart mouth, kid," he said pleasantly, "or I'll have to wash it out with soap."

"You and who else?" Lee's temper flared, but he cooled the effect of his words with a sheepish grin.

As if suddenly of one mind, the two men stepped closer to share a slightly embarrassed hug.

HOURS LATER, bags all packed and Jason sound asleep for the night, Thom T., Trey and Rachel sat around the kitchen table at the Rocking T, drinking coffee and talking. Anything to prolong the moment of parting, Trey thought morosely.

Tomorrow the Smith family would be up and out of here at first light. Thom T. wouldn't be left alone, however. Arrangements had been made for Kit Mc-Crae, another waif he'd befriended years before, to move to the ranch to keep him company. Trey had met her at the wedding and approved the choice.

Whatever remained to be said must be said now. They'd already agreed that no good purpose would be served by making public the truth about the Legend of Showdown.

"It's enough that we all know Rose ran away with Boone the Mysterious Gunfighter," Rachel reiterated. "Let the town keep its illusions—and the profit from Showdown Days."

"Suits me." Trey picked up his wife's hand and kissed her tender palm. "I wouldn't have minded being a Taggart *too* much, but hell! I've got everything else, so I won't complain."

Thom T.'s expression grew sly. "That reminds me," he said a little too innocently. Reaching inside his shirt, he withdrew an envelope, which he handed to Trey. "I got this in the mail today. It's the last of the stuff that detective dug up."

Why bother about it now? Puzzled, Trey glanced at Rachel, who raised her brows and shrugged. She didn't appear to know what this was all about, but Trey sensed her interest as he extracted three pieces of paper.

The first was a note from the detective's widow, advising Thom T. that she was sure this was the last of the material her husband had collected before his death.

The second was a birth certificate, issued by the State of Louisiana on the occasion of the birth of one Thomas Trenton Taggart Smith to John Taggart Smith and Linda Trenton Smith of New Orleans.

"Trey," Thom T. said, his eyes gleaming with excitement. "Trey for the three initials—*tres*—just like his great-great-grandpa come to be called Jeb for *his* initials—Jeremy Edward Boone Smith."

Trey felt as if someone had yanked the rug out from under him. Could it be true? After all they'd been through, could it be true? Suddenly helpless, he looked to Rachel for confirmation.

Tears streamed down her cheeks. "Oh, my God! Trey, you're a Taggart!"

"I...I can't believe..." Too choked up to say any more, Trey picked up the third piece of paper and stared at it without comprehension. Rachel took it gently from his hands.

But when she'd read the page and still said nothing, he glanced at her in question. She looked completely stunned.

He'd known it was too good to be true. Whatever she held in her hands must give the lie to the other documents.

"What is it?" he croaked.

"It's a memo," she whispered. "Your father died in 1975, leaving everything he owned in a trust fund for his son, *should he ever be located*. Trey, your father didn't abandon you! He couldn't find you! Apparently your mother took off with you when you were just an infant, while your father was out to sea. Darling, do you realize what this means?"

Thom T. and Rachel were both looking at him. Trey licked dry lips. "It means," he began slowly, "that I really am a Taggart. And I guess it means somebody loved me all along."

Blindly he reached out with both hands, one covering his wife's and the other the gnarly fist of the kind and generous old man who'd made everything possible. Overcome with emotion, he tried to deal with the realization that he, a bad boy from the Eastern slums, had finally laid the past to rest and found happiness—in *Texas*, of all places.

Thom T. smiled as if he understood.

"Kinda boggles your mind, don't it, boy?" the old man asked with a chuckle. "You've come a helluva long way and turned into a helluva man . . . for a damn Yankee!"

*   *   *   *   *

*Ruth Jean Dale's Taggarts of Texas continues!
Daniel Boone Taggart has his story in
Showdown!—Harlequin Romance #3242,
January 1993. And the truth about the
mysterious gunfighter and the legend of
Showdown, Texas, is revealed in Legend!—
Harlequin Historical #168, April 1993.*

A Note from Ruth Jean Dale

I like men with a sense of humor, men who don't take themselves too seriously. I like men who are secure in their masculinity and feel no need to prove anything to anybody. I especially like men who are comfortable laughing at their own foibles.

Trey Smith is such a man. He's also a loner, a risk-taker living on the edge. He's got nothing to lose ... except his life, which doesn't seem all that valuable to him. So how does Trey react when a rich but crusty old rancher from some dinky little town in Texas shows up claiming instant kinship? How does Trey like being labeled a "damn yankee" and falling in love with a woman who values public opinion as much as he disdains it?

Finding out was the fun of writing Trey's story. Along with the citizens of Showdown, Texas, I learned that although Trey Smith is a Yankee, he's a *red-blooded* Yankee. And Trey discovers something, too—the power of love: love of family, of community, and most of all, love of a very special woman. And *that's* what heroes are all about.

This month's irresistible novels from

THE RED-BLOODED YANKEE by Ruth Jean Dale

Meet Trey Smith—the last in Temptation's sinfully sexy line-up of men under the banner Rebels & Rogues. Footloose and fancy-free. He didn't give a damn what people said about him. Rachel Cox—the proper small-town librarian who knew from bitter experience that her reputation mattered. She couldn't afford to get involved with a man like Trey Smith!

MAIL ORDER MAN by Roseanne Williams

Jessie Patton had no time for romance. With her plain looks she knew she would never attract a man. Then her grandfather started placing personal ads...

STAR-CROSSED LOVERS by JoAnn Ross

Bram Starbuck's scientist friends dismissed his theories on space travel, but they wouldn't after he returned from Earth. Only something went wrong, he ended up in the wrong place, wrong century—but with the *right* woman.

WINNER TAKES ALL by Sharon Mayne

Steele Erickson and Bailey Richards each had their own reasons for wanting to infiltrate a gambling ring. The sting operation Bailey proposed would have her playing mistress to Steele's high-stakes roller—and Steele was determined they would do a lot more than playacting...

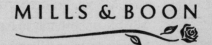

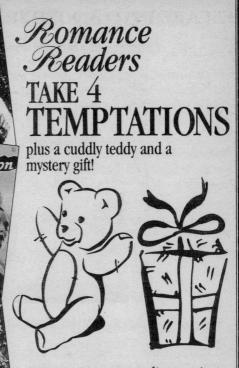

Romance Readers
TAKE 4 TEMPTATIONS
plus a cuddly teddy and a mystery gift!

We're inviting you to discover just why our Temptation series has become so popular with romance readers. You can enjoy 4 exciting Temptations as a free gift from Mills & Boon Reader Service, along with the opportunity to have 4 brand new titles delivered to your door every month!

TURN THE PAGE FOR DETAILS OF HOW TO CLAIM YOUR FREE GIFTS

A Tempting FREE Offer
from Mills & Boon

We'd love you to become a regular reader of Temptations and discover the modern sensuous love stories that have made this such a very popular series. To welcome you we'd like you to have 4 TEMPTATION books, a CUDDLY TEDDY and a MYSTERY GIFT absolutely FREE.

Then, each month you could look forward to receiving 4 brand new Temptations, delivered to your door, postage and packing FREE. Plus our free Newsletter full of author news, competitions, special offers and much more.

It's easy. Send no money now.
Simply fill in the coupon below and send it to-
Reader Service, FREEPOST, PO Box 236, Croydon, Surrey CR9 9EL.

No Stamp Required

Free Books Coupon

Yes! Please rush me 4 FREE Temptations and 2 FREE gifts! Please also reserve me a Reader Service subscription. If I decide to subscribe I can look forward to receiving 4 Temptations for just £7.40 each month, postage and packing FREE. If I decide not to subscribe I shall write to you within 10 days. I can keep the free books and gifts whatever I choose. I may cancel or suspend my subscription at any time. I am over 18 years of age.

Ms/Mrs/Miss/Mr_____ EP58 T

Address _____

_____

Postcode _____ Signature _____